THE WEIGHT OF WHAT CAME BEFORE

Jessica Lipani

CONTENTS

Title Page
Content Warning
Copyright
Dedication
Prologue — 1
Chapter 1 - The Stranger Who Knows My Name — 4
Chapter 2 - The Pull — 12
Chapter 3 - Held together by Deadlines — 14
Chapter 4 - The Space Between Balconies — 16
Chapter 5 - Games in The Dark — 20
Chapter 6 - Bruises and Red Flags — 27
Chapter 7 - Into the Lion's Den — 31
Chapter 8 - Business or Pleasure? — 38
Chapter 9 - Fire At My Door — 42
Chapter 10 - Lines Already Crossed — 48
Chapter 11 - The Man Behind The Curtain — 53
Chapter 12 - Dancing with the devil — 62
Chapter 13 - Unknown Number — 72
Chapter 14 - The Lines We Cross — 79
Chapter 15 - Into The Web — 84
Chapter 16 - A Taste of Control — 87

Chapter 17 - Crossing the Threshold	90
Chapter 18 - Caught In The Middle	96
Chapter 19 - Bound By The Fire	101
Chapter 20 - Tangled In Him	108
Chapter 21 – The Thing's I don't Say	115
Chapter 22 - The Mask Slips	120
Chapter 23 - The Cost Of Knowing Him	127
Chapter 24 - When Everything Changes	138
Chapter 25 – Old Instincts, New Rules	146
Chapter 26 - When The Past Starts Breathing Again	151
Chapter 27 - The Warning	161
Chapter 28 - When The Past Rears Its Ugly Head	165
Chapter 29 – I Won't Let Her Walk Alone	171
Chapter 30 - The Confrontation	174
Chapter 31 - Holding The Fragile Parts	181
Chapter 32 - Into The Fire With Open Eyes	188
Acknowledgement	193
About The Author	195

CONTENT WARNING

This book explores themes of survival, trauma and recovery following an abusive relationship. It contains references to domestic violence, stalking, psychological manipulation and physical injury. Some scenes may be distressing for readers sensitive to these topics

Copyright © 2026 Jessica Lipani

All rights reserved

The characters and events portrayed in this book are fictitious. Any similarity to real persons, living or dead, is coincidental and not intended by the author.

No part of this book may be reproduced, or stored in a retrieval system, or transmitted in any form or by any means, electronic, mechanical, photocopying, recording, or otherwise, without express written permission of the publisher.

ISBN: 9798278190400

To my Dad,
Who still whispers Gioia Mia to my heart when I forget who I am.
I Miss You.

This book is for everyone who has rebuilt themselves from the pieces someone else broke.
For every survivor who learned that desire and danger can speak the same language.
For the version of you that still looks over your shoulder.
For anyone who has ever loved dangerously, healed quietly or rebuilt themselves in the dark when no one was watching.
For the hearts that kept beating through chaos, for the strength found in silence and for the courage it takes to begin again, even when the past still echoes.

This is for you.

PROLOGUE

Tyler

She has no idea I'm here.

She's sitting alone outside at one of the metal tables, sunglasses pushed into her hair, tapping on her phone like she's trying to make the world make sense again.

I knew the name before the woman. Cass Palazzo.

The kind of reputation that travels quietly in the property industry; efficient, sharp and reliable. Exactly the sort of person you headhunt before someone else realises her value, which is how I came to know the name.

Her CV landed on my desk earlier this week and to be perfectly honest, on paper it was simple, she would be a perfect addition to Sparks Developments. In reality, she's chaos wrapped in soft skin and now I've seen her like this, raw and hungover, I can't separate the two.

Chicago's is my club. Not in the way people imagine, I don't hover or micromanage, but nothing moves through that place without my say so.

Her booking crossed my screen yesterday morning. Late reservation for a party of four and at the time it barely registered it was the same person.

Last night, she was a wildfire, dancing carelessly in her dress and heels, throwing herself around the dancefloor at Chicago's like she had nothing to lose.

She had no idea she was right under my nose.

She didn't notice the looks or the recalculations. The moment one of them decided she might be worth the trouble.

I noticed.

When he followed her outside, I stepped in. I stepped in because I wanted to. A gentle reminder. A look that told him he'd mis-read the situation. He backed off and that was enough.

That's the thing about desire, people think it's romantic. It isn't. It's feral. It doesn't ask, it just arrives and takes up space until you either feed it or kill it.

The door swings open and Gia almost walks straight into me.

"Jesus, Tyler," she mutters, clutching the tray to her chest. "You trying to give me a heart attack?"

"Relax, Gia," I barely look at her, my gaze still glued to Cass as she taps the lighter against the table. "You got her order?"

"Yeah," she says, voice softening. "Tea and a Bacon sarnie."

I smirk. Of course, the perfect hangover comfort food.

"Put it on my tab," I tell her.

She hesitates, her eyes flicker from me to the woman outside. "She one of yours?"

I don't answer that because I don't know how to. Instead, I push the door open and step into the crisp morning air.

Cass shivers, rubbing her arms as if she misjudged the weather. A faint crease has settled between her brows that wasn't there last night. Her eyes are hazel, the kind that never seem to settle on one colour, shifting between green and gold depending on the mood or the light, her mouth made for trouble and bad decisions, pursed tightly.

She pulls a cigarette out of the pack with her teeth and lights it. She shouldn't smoke, she shouldn't walk home alone at night, and she definitely shouldn't trust men who look at her the way I am right now.

If she knew who I was, what I am to this City, she'd run. At least, the sensible side would, but the problem is, there's something I've seen in her that doesn't always listen to the sensible part.

My phone buzzes in my pocket. A message from James flashes up.

'Boss, we got an issue with the shipment. Call me when you can.'

I slide my phone away without reading the rest of the message. Whatever the issue is, it can wait a little longer.

Right now, there's a woman outside with last night stamped to her face and her name already halfway out my mouth.

She probably thinks last night was a mistake, that it means nothing, just a forgettable evening with a string of messy choices.

She has no idea how wrong she is.

I didn't come looking for her, but I know when opportunity presents itself.

CHAPTER 1 - THE STRANGER WHO KNOWS MY NAME

The sun assaults my eyes as I step out of the cab: this is the *last* time I agree to breakfast with Lola after a night of overindulging in cocktails.

The cafe is already bustling, the sound of clinking cups and low chatter spilling out onto the pavement. I make a beeline for a lone space on a table outside before another smug face gets there first.

Dropping into the chair, a wave of nausea washes over me.

I check my phone. No missed calls. No messages from Lola. Just a missed call from late last night.

Blocked number.

With a sigh, I set my cigarettes and lighter on the table, resisting the urge to light one up immediately.

I rest my head against the cold metal chair and last night's memories flash back in my mind. Strobe lights, the sticky floor beneath my heels, the blur of faces as I danced harder than I have in months.

If the old ladies at the next table could see the mental slideshow currently playing, they'd probably drag me down the high street, ringing a bell, chanting *"Shame."*

Ten minutes ago, in the safety of my own flat, I convinced

myself that everything was fine, that last night was just another story to add to the mix. Now, under daylight that's far too bright, with the weight of a hangover pressing behind my eyes, it feels more like proof that my life is drifting slightly off course.

My head throbs in agreement. I rub at my temples but all it does is smear last nights eyeliner.

Where are the waitresses? They're like mystical creatures, never there when you need one, always hovering when you're mid-bite.

I study the menu. "A tea please, and a bacon sandwich," I rehearse, because apparently even ordering food with a hangover needs to be practiced.

The door swings open and one of the waitresses, Gia, I think, comes out with a tray, hips swaying. I lift my hand to catch her attention.

"Tea and a bacon sandwich please." Well done me.

"Of course love, coming right up."

Turning on her heels, as she finishes scribbling down my order, she saunters back through the door as swiftly as she came.

Moments later, the bell to the door chimes again and my eyes fall on an arm extending from the inside. A tanned, muscular arm. Veins. A watch that looks expensive in a subtle *'I definitely paid full price for this kind of way.'*

"Cheers Gia."

His voice is deep and effortless. The kind of voice that slips under your skin and settles there before you have a chance to stop it. The sound sends a shiver down my spine, distracting me from my flaring indigestion.

I lean back slightly, partly to see whose voice matches that arm, and partly because I've never had much control when curiosity is involved…and he is not what I expected.

You know some guys look good until they open their mouths?

He's the opposite. The voice was the warning, the face is the problem.

He's younger than the voice implied, late twenties maybe, early thirties at most.

He steps fully into view and the rest of him follows with quiet authority. Tall and broad-shouldered, built in a way that makes the clothes he wears look like they were made for him alone. His hair is dark, with subtle hints of silver running through it, a little unruly, like he didn't waste much time perfecting it because he doesn't need to.

His jaw is sharp enough to make me swallow, dusted with stubble that looks deliberate, like he knows what it does to people.

His green eyes flash with mischief. He possesses gaze that doesn't skim, *it pins.* When they land on me, they don't flick away. They hold, unhurried, as if he has all the time in the world to take me in.

There's an edge to him, and my body reacts before my brain can interfere.

Shit. His eyes lock onto mine and I lean back into my seat. His lips curl into a slow smirk, and I know straightaway I've been caught, there's no point pretending otherwise.

The one day my hair is screaming for help in a lopsided bun, with a hangover from hell flooding out of my pores, I stumble across him.

I fumble for my cigarettes, pulling one out, but my lighter clicks uselessly three times before finally lighting the flame.

I inhale too quickly and the smoke hits the back of my throat like a punch. I cough, blinking through watering eyes, dignity evaporating in real time.

Then I feel him. Not touching me, just there. A quiet, undeniable presence at my side calling for my attention, whether I like it or not.

"It's a bad habit, you know."

"Hurh, what?" I splutter. *Smooth Cass.*

I drag my gaze up to meet his, bracing myself for whatever mess of a conversation my brain's about to patch together.

Up close, his eyes are sharper, playful, like he's three steps ahead in a conversation we are yet to have.

"Smoking," his eyes flit to the cigarette. "Rough morning?"

A sudden hangover jitter shoots through me, and the ash from the cigarette drops straight onto my white trousers.

"For fuck's sake," I hiss, batting at the grey smear spreading across my leg. "That obvious?" I croak.

"The sun is brutal today," he says mildly. "Doesn't show much mercy after Chicago's."

"How do you…" I begin before clamping my mouth shut. Did I meet him last night? Surely I'd remember him, unless I was more drunk than I thought.

My phone is still stubbornly silent on the table. No message. No Lola. Now she's late for breakfast and I'm alone with a stranger who somehow knows what club I go to.

"I own the place."

"You own Chicago's?"

A corner of his mouth lifts. "Amongst other things."

He doesn't elaborate; he doesn't need to. There's confidence in his manner, as if he's stating a fact rather than something to be impressed by.

"Do you make a habit of tracking down your customers the morning after?"

His gaze flicks to the empty chair opposite. "Only the interesting ones."

Bright red waving flag.

"Oh, I'm waiting for someone," I blurt, because apparently, it's very important that this stranger knows I'm not a complete loser.

Shards of last night flash through my mind, still wondering if I had seen him at the bar.

Nope. I sure as hell would remember that face.

Gia appears then, tray balanced on one hip. "Tea and bacon sarnie for..." She pauses, glancing between us.

"Cass," he says calmly.

My name lands between us like he's been saving it.

"How do you know my name?"

He doesn't answer straight away, like he's measuring the moment.

"Your booking," he says finally. "From last night. Late reservation for a party of four."

"Oh," I mutter, feeling ridiculous for being relieved. Of course, that makes sense.

I stand too quickly and my chair scrapes harshly against the floor. "I should probably...pay for my stuff."

"You're good," he says casually. "Already paid."

Of course, the ridiculously attractive stranger who knows my name and my hangover history, also pays my bill like it's nothing.

"Well, I'm glad to have made an impression," I say cooly, escaping inside to get a takeaway cup.

My irritation should win. Instead, something treacherous in me warms.

It wasn't that he knew my name; it was the way he'd waited to use it.

~

My flat is small, but new. Two bedrooms with a large balcony overlooking a neat courtyard below. My neatly displayed crystals and warm lighting make it feel safe. I worked hard for this place. Long hours in an industry full of men who thought I should be grateful for a basic response.

Promotions came from hard work, sweat and some blood.

Lola calls me boring for working so much, and maybe she's right, but boring pays the bills.

I glance at my reflection in the balcony door and pause. Olive skin, courtesy of Father, warm even in the low light. Mousey brown hair falling loosely and imperfect past my shoulders, fringe skimming my brows

I'm no Lola. No endless legs or glossy hair that turns heads without effort. No parade of admirers trailing behind me like a hobby, but I never struggle for dinner invitations either.

They just never seem to go anywhere.

Finally, I'm curled up on my sofa in clean pyjamas, after a hot bath that washed away most of my shame.

I'm almost convinced that this morning was nothing, just an odd encounter.

I haul myself off the sofa and pour a generous glass of red wine. A night-cap.

My ID and bank card are still missing, so I've reported them as lost, another small inconvenience I could do without tonight.

Stepping onto the balcony, armed with my cigarettes and wine, the cool evening air welcomes me.

The shrill ringing of the house phone startles me, but I ignore it. It's Bea, my sister, checking if I'm indoors on a Saturday night.

My family is complicated. I keep my distance, a comfortable hour drive away, sharing only the highlights they need to know about.

I prop my feet up on the chair opposite, take another swig of wine and cast my eyes across the balconies of my neighbours.

Lighting a cigarette, the smoke fills my lungs, as my eyes scan the balconies opposite. Most are dark, with only a few illuminated by a light or a TV playing. I've never met any of my neighbours, and honestly, that suits me. The less people know about my life, the better.

A figure steps onto the balcony directly across from mine, barely lit by a faint glow from inside. He's mostly shadowed at first, a tall silhouette against the low light. I really wish I'd turned off my lights. Surely, he can't see where I'm looking... right?

A couple walks through the courtyard below, triggering the sensor lights, giving me a clearer view of the man.

Holy. Shit.

The figure leans forward over the railing, bare-chested in the cool night air, V-lines disappearing into low-slung jeans, that sit as if they were never meant to stay there.

The day has been one long tease. First the stranger at the cafe, now this. Do all the hot men in this city hide away and only emerge on one day of the year?

I lean forward for a better view, forgetting about the wine glass nestled in my lap and it crashes to the floor, shattering loudly, sending shards of glass in every direction.

"Shit!" I yelp, jumping to my feet.

When I look up, the balcony opposite is empty, and the figure's vanished, swallowed back into the darkness behind the curtains.

Adrenaline fizzes under my skin.

I retreat inside and shut the balcony door, the click of the latch louder than it ought to be, my skin still humming with the sense of being seen.

In bed, I run my fingertips along the raised scar at the back of my neck, just as I always do when my thoughts begin to spiral. Old memories start to surface, but I push them down.

I'm not that girl anymore.

I close my eyes and the day rewinds itself in fragments. The cafe. The stranger. The balcony. The way my chest tightened when he said my name like he'd known it for years.

Across the courtyard, behind sheer curtains, Tyler runs a hand through his wet hair and smirks. She reacted exactly how he hoped.

CHAPTER 2 - THE PULL

The stranger from the cafe doesn't leave my head when I wake up. He shouldn't be there at all.

My headache has downgraded from 'death is close' to 'do not speak to me louder than a whisper.' Anything is progress I suppose.

I squeeze my eyes shut but his face creeps in anyway. Sharp smile, the confidence in how he claims he owns Chicago's, as casually as if he were talking about the weather. The way he watched me, as if he were taking down my blueprint, like he could now rebuild me from memory alone.

My phone buzzes on the side.

Blocked caller.

I ignore the call and wait for it to ring out.

The sun creeps higher, streaking through the courtyard, lighting up my balcony, signalling that the morning has arrived whether I like it or not.

My phone buzzes again.

Lola: *You alive? Xx*

I let out a huff.

Me: *Barely, where were you yesterday morning? Why haven't you answered my calls?*

Three dots appear, disappear and reappear again.

Lola: Overslept x

My phone buzzes again almost immediately.

Lola: Overslept with a delicious man in my bed that made it too hard to leave. I'm sorry x

I roll my eyes, of course.

Part of me envies her, the way she navigates life without overthinking or building walls first.

The coffee machine beeps, pulling me back to my kitchen. I take my freshly brewed hit of adrenaline with me to the shower, the aroma clinging to the air, and suddenly I'm back at the cafe.

Get it together Cass.

I lock my phone, placing it on my kitchen counter like the action alone might lock him out of my mind too.

CHAPTER 3 - HELD TOGETHER BY DEADLINES

The office is too bright, noisy and full of men who need things from me before I've had my coffee. I'm barely through the door when Jack, one of the Directors, waves a stack of client folders at me.

"Cass, finally. We've got a mess over at Fairfield Village. Contract disputes, delays, nothing's on track. You'll need to go through these as soon as possible."

Of course I do. I always do.

I force a polite smile. "Morning to you too, Jack."

He drops the files on my desk with a thud that stirs the thin film of dust behind my computer screen into a brief, shimmering cloud.

"Palazzo, you're the only one who can work through this," he says with his back turned, already retreating into his office, like a sailor abandoning his sinking ship.

Exhaling sharply, I shove my bag under the table.

Immersing myself into my newly assigned workload feels easier than sitting with the lingering haze of anxiety stirred by that stranger from the cafe, a nagging feeling that he knew more than what he was letting on.

Work is therapy; it acts as a good distraction...well, mostly.

By lunchtime, both cups of coffee I made still sit untouched on my desk.

I pinch the bridge of my nose, trying to ward off the familiar sensation of an oncoming headache.

"Cass, you still with us?"

Rachael plops herself into the chair beside me, crossing one leg over the other in her tailored cream suit. She looks sharp, younger than her forty-three years.

"You look....tense," she says gently.

"I've had better days," I huff.

"Long night?" Her eyebrows lift questioningly.

"Not like that," a chuckle escapes me.

Her lips twitch with amusement. "Okay, but you should take a break. You look like you need one."

I check my phone for the fourth time that hour, no more blocked calls, but my stomach still twists.

"I'm alright for now," I lie.

Rachael's gaze lingers on me and her face softens. "You know... people see how much you take on and forget you're human. You're too helpful."

Anthony from finance appears hastily, rapping his fingers on my desk.

"Cass, can you come look at the budget discrepancies for the new build. Nothing will move forward until they're agreed."

I shoot Rachael a look and she grimaces on my behalf.

"Go," she sighs, "but take that break after!"

Tonight, I'll go home, cook dinner and pretend everything is normal. Tonight is going to be a normal evening.

I decide that firmly enough that I almost believe it.

CHAPTER 4 - THE SPACE BETWEEN BALCONIES

After four days of brutal early mornings and even later nights, washing the dishes feels therapeutic, the kind of task that demands absolutely nothing from me except existing.

My phone buzzes for the sixth minute straight and I finally dry my hands and pick it up.

Lola. She's been getting under my skin a little lately. I mean, I love her obviously, but it's like she's playing hard to get with me.

When the phone rings again, I flop onto the sofa and answer on the last ring.

"Cass, I'm sorry! I miss you and we need to talk about everything. I'm a little… caught up right now, but wanted to check in."

A man's voice whispers in the background. I roll my eyes and shift my phone to my other ear.

"Tomorrow. Be ready for 8 p.m. I'm coming over and I want to know every ounce of gossip from tonight."

"Bring prosecco," I say smirking.

"You love me, see you tomorrow!" she giggles, followed by the muffled sound of her telling some man to stop whatever he was up to, before the line goes dead.

I let my phone drop onto my stomach, as I still lay sprawled across my sofa.

Friday's Tinder date flashes back to me and I cringe. Ten minutes... that's all it took for me to realise I'd been lured into dinner with an obnoxious weasel, masquerading as a 'property professional'.

His profile picture suggested dimples, a dog dad and wholesome Sunday walks. The reality, however, was a man who couldn't keep his eyes off the waitress's arse long enough to look at the menu.

Lola has always warned me that a man who flips his phone upside-down has something to hide. Turns out she was right. She's insufferable when she's right.

Dragging myself upright, I pour a glass of wine and open my laptop, the universal tools of avoidance.

Thanks to Lola's relentless encouragement, I have a date tonight but, after my previous experience, hope is hanging by a thread.

I try responding to emails, but after ten minutes my brain rejects the responsibility entirely. A Facebook notification blinks in the corner of the screen and I succumb without hesitation.

Meal pictures. Babies. Holiday updates. Engagement announcements.

I'm seconds from shutting the laptop when a photo at the top of my feed catches my eye, posted by a girl I briefly worked with. She's standing with a group of friends, captioned:

So ready for another night like this at @SparksRooftopBar tomorrow.

I scroll through the smiling faces and freeze.

It's him. The guy from the cafe.

My pulse pounds at the base of my throat.

It's been nearly a week, and for reasons I can't fully explain, I still haven't managed to get him out of my mind.

I tried googling Chicago's earlier in the week to find out his name, but I couldn't find anything useful or interesting.

I enlarge the photo instinctively. He's dressed casually, dark jeans and a fitted T-shirt that stretches across his chest and shoulders, the fabric moulding around his muscular biceps and tanned skin. In his left hand, he holds a motorbike helmet.

Of course he rides a bike.

My mind bubbles with excitement as I hover over his annoyingly perfect face, irritation flaring when I see there's no tagged profile.

I bookmark the page on my browser before my brain can talk me out of it, purely for investigative purposes.

Clicking on the tagged business 'Sparks Rooftop Bar', I browse through their photos and there he is again, standing beside another man at the bar, arms slung around each other, both grinning at the camera. My heart skips a beat.

Glancing at the time, it's already 6:30pm and with a snap, I shut the laptop.

Grabbing my cigarettes, I step onto the balcony, tiptoeing around the stray shards of glass I still haven't properly cleaned.

Note to self: clean the bloody balcony before a shard lodges itself in my foot.

I flick my gaze across the courtyard to the balcony opposite and I'm a little disappointed at its emptiness. No sign of the alluring stranger from the other night.

I inhale deeply, tilting my head back towards the sky. Stars scatter in every direction, forming patterns I wish I knew the names of. The night is cool and calming, and for a moment I close my eyes and simply exist.

I take a final pull of my cigarette and stub it out, then step back inside. Before shutting the balcony door, I sneak a last glance at the flat opposite.

For a second, I swear the curtains shift. My eyes catch the faintest ripple of movement, as if someone on the other side had just shifted their weight.

I blink, but curtains don't move again.

With a quiet sigh, I retreat back through the door, gently closing it behind me. Whether I like it or not, I have to get ready for tonight's date.

Across the courtyard, the light goes out.

CHAPTER 5 - GAMES IN THE DARK

What a waste of a perfectly good outfit, I should have left ten minutes ago.

The restaurant is one of those pretentious 'modern' places; exposed brick, dimly lit with long single lights hanging from the ceiling, making me feel as though I'm at a sensory experience rather than a date. It's one of those places developers and financiers loved: overpriced, dramatic and just close enough to Sparks Rooftop to feel exclusive.

Every table is dressed in gold cutlery and the water glasses are deliberately slanted, making it feel as though your face is having a stroke every time you take a sip of water. The kind of place you take someone to impress them.

Soft music plays under the clatter of plates. Candles flicker between courses and it smells of rosemary and truffle oil.

I'm not completely present. I keep scanning the room without meaning to, not for him, I tell myself, just for something familiar.

I stab at my phone.

"Lola, it's me. Why do you never answer when I actually need you? Call me back. Please. Fake an emergency so I can get out of this date. If I stay any longer, I'm going to fall asleep and headbutt the table."

I hang up and immediately regret every life choice that led me here, instead of being curled up in my flat with my blanket and favourite wine. Leaning against the wall outside the restaurant toilets, I release a long, frustrated exhale.

Lola told me once, after my breakup with Jake, that *'I'm chronically attracted to charm over character.'* She's not entirely wrong; watching too many rom-coms over the years may have caused some confusion. Broad men with commanding voices and smouldering looks, making them sound like gods, not men.

A voice cuts through the hallway.

"Unless he's an absolute moron," a familiar voice drawls behind me, "he's going to know you're not feeling the date."

I turn slowly.

The man from the cafe leans against the opposite wall like he owns the shadows, his brows lifting slightly as his eyes meet mine, like this wasn't where he expected to find me.

For a moment, my mouth opens, but no words manage to come out.

He tilts his head, rolling his eyes. "Come on. Faking emergencies? It's one of the oldest tricks in the book and this place isn't cheap, you know."

I gather what's left of my dignity. "Is eavesdropping a hobby of yours, or do you just stalk people at their favourite places to eat?"

He pushes off the wall, stepping into better light and my irritation stumbles over the sight of him. Dark suit, no tie, crisp shirt slightly open at the collar. He looks even better than he did at the cafe. Sharp and handsome in a way that should be illegal.

"Are you checking me out Cass?" His mouth curves upwards.

My chest flares crimson. "Get over yourself. It's weird that you know my name and I don't have a clue who you are."

The toilet door swings open, giving me an escape. "You go," I tell him quickly. "I have to get back. My date is probably wondering where I am."

Making his way towards the toilet door, his mouth twitches. "I'm sure he is and who knows…if you manage to stay awake, you might even enjoy yourself."

I glare at him and he chuckles, then disappears inside.

He smiles like he planned this.

I make my way back to the table where my date is sipping his drink

"Sorry, there was a queue."

"Oh, that's okay! You know, there was this one time I had to wait in a queue and…"

His voice dissolves into background noise as I glance at my phone again. Come on, Lola. Save me.

I tune back in just long enough, as I refill my wine glass, to catch on about something involving a neighbour, a step and a long queue.

Handsome cafe man catches my eye as he walks past our table, smirking while glancing at my date and then back at me, raising an eyebrow.

A warning? I can't tell, but my body reacts like it's been struck.

Throwing my head back, I burst into laughter. "Oh, that really is hilarious."

Oh no," he says slowly, "she really does have to wear an eye patch now."

Mortified, I shove wine into my mouth to hide my burning cheeks and look anywhere but at him.

I glance across the restaurant and my eyes find *him* with ease. He fits in here too perfectly, almost effortlessly, like he was carved to sit in dimly lit places with expensive wine.

I pick at my food, as my date rambles on, all whilst my eyes drift repeatedly to the stranger without meaning to.

Then, he turns and raises his wine glass towards me, gesturing, and his entire table looks over.

Well, this is incredibly fucking awkward.

I quickly divert my gaze, set my cutlery down, and pretend my date is suddenly the most fascinating man alive.

Panic swells in my chest like a fast tide as I sense him stand, his footsteps edging closer.

"Should we go?" I blurt, as Liam cuts through his steak, oblivious.

"Cass, is that you?"

No. No, no, no.

I offer a smile as my date glances up and acknowledges our new company.

He steps between the tables. "Cass, it's been ages. It's me. Tyler. From college. How've you been, toot?"

Is that his name?

My date looks between us, bewildered. "Toot?"

Tyler offers his hand, shaking Liam's firmly. "Old habit. It was my nickname for her back in the day."

Before I can protest, he casually drops into the empty sofa seat beside me and nudges my shoulder.

"We dated briefly," he says smoothly. "Cass had a thing for boats. Well…captains, really. Getting them to toot their horns. Swinging came after."

My jaw hits the floor.

Tyler glances at me and winks. WINKS.

"I was very territorial," he adds casually. "Swinging wouldn't have worked for me. Anyway, that was ages ago. How long have you two been together?"

Liam fidgets in his seat, noticeably uncomfortable.

"Oh, it's our first date actually," he replies, scratching the back of his head. "Sorry, I err just need to use the bathroom."

He grabs his jacket, darting towards the back of the restaurant.

I turn my whole body towards Tyler, "Swinging? Fucking Swinging? You're honestly a right pain in my arse."

He shrugs, smirking. "It was the first thing that came to mind."

"I was right," I snap. "Meddling is your hobby." I raise an eyebrow at him and press my lips together firmly.

He leans in slightly. "Come on, Toot. Lighten up. You weren't going to end up with him."

He reaches forward, taking my wine glass like he owns it and drinks from it.

"Mmm," his tongue grazes his lips. "Good taste… expensive taste."

I snatch the glass back, seething and not nearly drunk enough, whilst I scan the room for signs of my fleeing date.

Tyler raises an eyebrow, amused. "Oh, he left. Slipped out when he thought we weren't looking. Real gentleman, leaving you with the bill." His eyes sweep across the restaurant.

Before I can respond, he catches my hand and gently raises it to his lips, heat coursing up my arm, while his eyes never leave mine. I should pull away, but I don't. He releases my hand and I think I've forgotten how to breathe.

His gaze flicks towards his own table and the brunette is staring at us, white knuckled fingers clenched around the stem of her wine glass.

Tyler straightens his suit jacket. "I should get back, but thank you for making my night… memorable."

He pulls our four crisp £50 notes from his wallet and places them neatly on the table. "No girl of mine pays the bill."

I push the money back towards him with a sharp glare and stand up.
"I'm not one of your girls," I say coolly, nodding at the brunette without breaking eye contact.

I walk past him towards the bar to settle the bill, heat prickling between my shoulder blades from where his gaze remains fixed.

As I'm nearing the exit, something compels me to look back.

Tyler raises his glass towards me, slow and deliberate; a silent challenge written in the curl of his mouth.

What a ridiculous waste of freshly shaved legs.

~

As I push through the doors into the cool night air, I glance over my shoulder again with a feeling I can't shake.

I scan the nearly empty road and my skin prickles. There's a couple waiting for a bus, a man smoking, leaning on the bus stop sign and a car idling across the street, but the weariness in my chest refuses to lift.

I walk towards the cab rank, footsteps quick but controlled. Every shadow puts me further on edge and every passing figure seems to linger a moment too long.

It's nothing. I'm imagining it. It's Tyler's fault, the adrenaline of my encounter with him but, halfway down the road, a figure catches my eye as I cross.

Far back enough to be nothing, but close enough to seem deliberate. I pick up my pace and dare not turn around fully.

Looking into the reflection of a shop window, I catch the faintest reflection of a tall figure following several paces behind me.

There isn't any rush or urgency in their walk; they are just close enough for me to hear the clip of their footsteps.

I swallow hard and step up to the kerb, raising my hand as a cab approaches. It pulls over fast, thank God.

I slide in as quickly as I can without appearing frantic and only then do I allow myself to look back.

The figure stops at the corner, watching.

CHAPTER 6 - BRUISES AND RED FLAGS

I swipe the last bit of mascara onto my lashes when my phone buzzes in the other room. I rush to snatch it up before it diverts to voicemail again.

"Cass," Lola's voice bursts through the speaker. "I'm on my way. I've got the prosecco to get us started…and I've got a little surprise…but I know you hate surprises, so I'll tell you when I arrive."

She hangs up before I get a chance to respond.

Dread creeps through me; I really do hate surprises.

Sighing, I leave my laptop open on my bed and rummage in the cupboard for two champagne flutes, bracing myself for whatever Lola considers a "surprise", which usually lands somewhere between chaos and catastrophe.

Before I even set them down, my spare keys rattle in the lock and in sweeps Lola, a whirlwind of perfume, shopping bags and untamed energy.

"So," she begins, eyeing my not quite finished face, "My surprise…" She pauses dramatically. "I've worked my magic and…we've got two passes to the event tonight at Chicago's!"

I blink. "That's the surprise? You vanish for days, stand me up for breakfast, and your apology gift is… a night out? Seriously, Lola." Heat flares in my chest. "At this point I'm just happy you're alive."

Her smile falters. "I'm sorry," she murmurs, reaching for my hands. Her fingers, normally warm, are shaking slightly.

Her eyes cloud over with guilt. "You know me. I meet someone, get caught up in the whole romantic bliss fantasy and then… well, here I am again."

She forces a small laugh that's brittle around the edges.

As she tucks a curl behind her ear, her sleeve slips back just enough for something dark to peek out from beneath the fabric.

A purple bruise. Some areas are old, while others are just blooming with new colour.

My stomach drops. "What's this?"

The bruise is worse than I expected, angry and finger-shaped.

"Jesus, Lola," the words scrape out of me.

She jerks back, tugging the fabric down as if hiding it could make me unsee it.

"Lola…" I breathe, but my throat is tight.

"I'm fine," she says too quickly. "It's nothing."

"You're not fine," I soften my tone. "Lola, what happened? Talk to me, let me help."

"It's sorted." Her voice is quiet but final.

She wipes at her eyes with the back of her sleeve, missing one tear that continues on its path toward her jaw.

"Sorted?" I repeat. "A bruise like that doesn't just…get sorted."

She looks at me and her expression softens. "Not tonight Cass. Please. Let's just have a good night."

She steps forward slightly. "We'll talk," she whispers. "Just… not now. Please."

She squeezes my arm with a smile that doesn't reach her eyes, turning away at a speed that almost sends me off balance, then pours two glasses of prosecco, filling them right to the top.

"Right now, I need a drink," she says brightly. "And as my best friend, I need you to get dressed and come out with me. I need to let loose."

She presses a glass into my hand. Her fingers still trembling, but before I can gather my thoughts, she darts into my bedroom, fleeing with all the urgency of animals in a wildfire.

I stand frozen in the doorway, the fizz in my glass rising and falling in tiny anxious bubbles.

Nothing. The same word she used that night I found her crying in a cheap hotel shower in Ibiza. She was nineteen, sunburnt, drunk and had mascara running down both cheeks.

A boy she hardly knew had thrown her phone into the sea during a boat party after accusing her of flirting. She lied then too. *'It's fine, Cass, he didn't mean it.'* I was the one who cuddled her whilst she sobbed in the shower against the cold tiles until the sun came up, whispering that we were going home.

A sharp gasp erupts from the other room. "WHO is that?"

Rushing in I find her leaning over my laptop, eyes wide with delight.

I'd forgotten to close my browser earlier, and the page I was stalking is still open with Tyler's face plastered across it.

I snap the laptop shut so fast she yelps.

"He's my friend," I say far too quickly. "He's gay."

Lola's eyes sparkle. "Let me see! Don't be such a prude."

"Nope. You already have enough straight men tripping over themselves."

She huffs, but drops it.

"Well, you're definitely not wearing any of these dresses," she announces, diving into my wardrobe like a woman possessed as my clothes fall to the floor in exhausted, crumpled heaps.

By the time I finish my drink, she's fishing out a rhinestone-covered mini dress from deep inside a shopping bag.

"This is for you. My formal apology," she reveals, thrusting it into my arms. "Try it on. I'm not taking no for an answer."

Alcohol hums pleasantly through my veins. "Fine…"

I pull the dress on, fasten the side and do up the little hook meant to secure it in place.

A stranger stares back at me from the mirror, shimmering and unreal.

"Where did you get the money for a dress like this?" I ask suspiciously.

Lola taps the side of her nose. "Don't question it."

She steps back, eyes widening, "Fucking hell Cass, where have you been hiding those curves!"

I turn to the mirror again. The silver rhinestones on the dress shimmer like stars caught in fabric. Those that hang off in strands, catch the light, creating an explosion of colour to dance around the room.

I don't recognise myself and maybe that's the point.

"Lola," I say slowly, "how about a change of plans?"

She meets my eyes through the mirror. "Go on."

"I think we should head to Sparks Rooftop. I've heard it's supposed to be a good night."

She pauses for a moment, just a flicker, but I notice it.

"Oh, lovely, sounds great. Let me get my stuff together."

As I adjust my hair in the mirror, I catch Lola's reflection behind me, her thumbs tapping rapidly on her phone, eyes sharp.

The bruise feels like the beginning of something I don't know how to stop.

CHAPTER 7 - INTO THE LION'S DEN

The cab rolls to a stop beside a narrow alley lit by a single flickering lamp. A discreet sign hangs above a heavy black door: **STAGE DOOR.**

Lola smooths her dress and flashes me a look over her shoulder. "I told you, I know the bouncer tonight. He'll get us in."

"You're sure you're not setting me up for a surprise performance?" I mutter. "Because I'm not going on stage for anyone."

My tummy does a little flip just as the door pops open.

Lola greets the hulking bouncer with fluttering eyes, showing him something on her phone. He nods once before waving us in. Lola smirks, tossing him a kiss over her shoulder.

I swallow the thread of unease weaving its way through me and follow her into a mirrored lift.

I catch my reflection as the doors close. The woman staring back at me looks like she belongs and I don't trust her.

Sparks Rooftop sits twenty-five floors above the city. As soon as we step out through the mirrored lift doors, I'm greeted by the majestic view of the skyline. The soft city lights glow in the distance, and the warm air envelops us, scented faintly with expensive aftershave and the heat of bodies pressed close together.

Nothing about Sparks feels accidental.

A marble bar adorns the right side of the room, lit from beneath so it glows a soft amber. Velvet sofas curve along the walls, creating private nooks for people to sit in, with seductive red casts from bulbs that are strung along the ceiling in a line.

In the centre of the room, several sculptural chandeliers hang from the ceiling, glistening in the light, like fireworks - fitting for a place called Sparks.

Lola flashes me a knowing grin and glides toward a lightly curtained off section.

A private bar gleams in the centre, crowded with well-dressed men and women who look as if they walked straight out of a magazine. A blonde woman with a sharp bob sings soft jazz into a vintage microphone, her voice transcending through the air like smoke.

The staff here are unnervingly polished; sharp monochrome outfits, women dressed in tailored satin, name badges that are sleek, almost hidden. They seem to move with quiet intention, gliding between tables with trained eyes.

Lola fits in without trying.

She grips my hand, her earlier worry melting into a wide smile.

"Lola?" We both turn.

A man approaches, tall, clean-shaven and extremely handsome, in a suit that fits too perfectly to be from the high street.

The moment Lola sees him, something in her relaxes.

Her shoulders soften and her smile widens. When he reaches her, he doesn't grab or pull her close, he simply plants a kiss on her cheek.

His gentle touch makes me soften inside; it can't be the man who left her bruised.

"Cass," Lola says radiantly. "This is James."

He smiles easily, perhaps a bit too easily for a place like this.

"Nice to finally meet you. Lola talks about you all the time."

I raise an eyebrow at her and she elbows me in warning.

As they speak, there's an unmistakable pull between them, subtle and unspoken.

He watches her like she's a book he's afraid to crease.

My brows knit. Lola hadn't said a word about him. Not one. She usually flaunts her conquests like new purchases, but this one? Hidden.

James leans down, whispering close to Lola's ear.
"Boss is here, he dropped by ten minutes ago. Said he's waiting for someone," he pauses. "Doesn't usually do that so it could mean trouble."

Lola's posture tightens in response and I don't like it.

"Come on girls, let's grab some drinks."

I trail behind them, but I don't get far because something catches my eye.

At the far end of the rooftop, near an unmarked door that blends into the wall, two men stand too stiffly to be regular workers, their demeanour too tough. One holds a clipboard he doesn't write on and the other grumbles into an earpiece discreetly.

They're not here for the bar.

Just as the door behind them cracks open, I hurry to catch up with Lola and James, but they're so wrapped up in each other that they don't even notice I've fallen behind.

"She's clever," James says quietly, nodding his head backwards as if signalling to me, "sharp, doesn't miss much, it's not going to be easy."

I hear every word.

I clear my throat and close the remaining distance, reaching for Lola's hand.

Letting James walk ahead, I tug Lola back slightly. "Promise me this wasn't him?" I whisper, signalling to her arm.

"No. No Cass," she cups my cheeks, her voice breaking. "This wasn't James." A weak smile dances across her face as she casts her eyes over to where James stands.

"Why didn't you tell me about him?" Hurt stings beneath my ribs.

"Cass, can we discuss this another time?" she begs again. "Not here. Not now. You don't always need to know every tiny detail."

I inhale shakily. "Fine."

She hesitates for a moment too long. "Let's get a drink."

~

It's well past midnight as I finally peel myself away from the shadowed booth where Lola and James sit tangled together, whispering and laughing.

My dress, gorgeous but torturous, has rhinestones digging into the backs of my thighs. I need a drink. One that doesn't come with polite conversation or third wheeling.

The music has shifted; the earlier soulful jazz has been replaced by a deep bass that vibrates up through the soles of my heels. Sparks has transformed into something darker as bodies move like waves on the dance floor.

I weave through the crowd towards the bar, hair falling down my back like a lure, lips parted just enough to catch the barman's eye and it works. His gaze drops to my neckline, his mouth pulling at a grin.

"Disaronno on the rocks and a sambuca shot," I ask, resting my elbows on the marble bar.

He pours, forearms flexing under rolled-up sleeves.

Still no sign of Tyler.

I take the shot, welcoming the burn like an old friend. The warmth blooms instantly in my chest, softening the edge of the night.

"These are on me," the bartender says with a cocky grin. "But only if you take a shot with me first."

He pours again, sliding the glass toward me before I can answer.

A deep, careless voice sounds behind me. "I think she's had enough for tonight."

The bartender's smirk fades from his face.

I roll my eyes, already feeling woozy from the sambuca. "When I buy my own drinks, I decide when I've had enough."

I don't bother looking at the arrogant stranger who killed my tiny moment of fun. I reach for my drink again, but when I look at the bartender, he's suddenly busy polishing glasses that don't need polishing.

Great.

His voice is closer this time, low and rough. "Rumour has it I make you nervous."

I turn too fast and the room tilts.

Strong hands catch the edges of my bar stool before I tip over, steadying me, hands welcomely skim my bare thighs.

"You," I manage.

Those striking green eyes catch the faint light, paired with his irresistibly handsome smirk that signals trouble, making my stomach flip uncontrollably.

Tyler's dressed in all black tonight; black trousers, a black fitted shirt rolled up to the elbows, exposing strong forearms and a simple belt pulling the outfit together. It's unfair how good he looks. The kind of good that should come with a warning label.

"I've spent all evening waiting for you to be alone," he coos, leaning in, claiming my space without even touching me.

"Seems you've had a good night," Tyler says softly. His fingers brush the skin just below my ear, as his thumb grazes my jaw, gentle enough for it not to feel like a threat.

I swallow hard as words gather on my tongue and die there.

He steps back just enough to look me over, running a hand through his tousled hair before folding his arms across his chest. His thumb drags slowly across his lower lip, his gaze never leaving mine.

My heart is pounding so hard I'm surprised the whole bar can't hear it.

"Let's get some air," he urges, "you might find your voice out there."

He extends his hand out towards me. His skin is rougher than I expected, worked and masculine, in a way that contradicts the polish of the venue.

Side by side, we walk towards the velvet curtains, the air thickening around us with each step, like the night itself is holding its breath and I notice the way the room shifts around him.

A waitress pauses what she's doing to hold open the door for Tyler. Beside her, a burly man in a suit murmurs into his earpiece before giving Tyler a brief nod, so subtle I almost convince myself I imagine it.

My breath slips out in a slow exhale.

Whatever this place is, I've already been noticed.

CHAPTER 8 - BUSINESS OR PLEASURE?

The night air bites against my bare skin and sharpens my senses. I'm aware of who I'm with and that I should leave, but I don't want to.

Tyler stands in front of me, hands in his pockets like he's waiting for something and my body leans towards him without permission.

I don't want him. I *shouldn't* want him. He's unpredictable and intense and every instinct I rely on goes haywire when he's close.

Fear and desire press against each other. "Has anyone ever told you that you're a dick?" I murmur.

His smile deepens. "Aren't most men?"

He lifts a hand, brushing a stray strand of hair behind my ear, but I don't move away. Tyler guides me in the direction of the rooftop bar that is mostly empty at this hour, leaving me on the edge of knowing that this could be dangerous.

"So, it's true," he says steadily, "I know more about you than you know about me, but we will get to that eventually."

He sets our drinks down and meets my eyes without flinching.

"I grew up around here," he says, "I know everyone, so I'm surprised to see you here."

I straighten up, fighting the flutter in my stomach.

"Maybe I got a tip off that you'd be here," I tease.

"Enjoy your date last night?"

My cheeks bruise with embarrassment.

"Why," I snap, regaining some composure, "did you have to be such an arse?"

His eyes flash. "Yeah, I am sorry about that. I got a little carried away."

His hand grazes my bare thigh, just above my knee and lingers. His touch is unexpected enough that I catch my breath, but instead of pulling back, warmth spreads through me. Part of me leans into it, craving more than I'm ready to admit.

His maddening smirk returns and he takes another slow sip of his drink.

I've spent years in places like this, surrounded by men who owned things, controlled everything and decided who stayed and who was…disposable.

Tyler fits easily here among them.

Not as a guest but as someone they answer to.

Tyler's eyes don't leave mine, observing my reactions.

"I have work in four hours," I say, sliding off the stool. "I should go, tonight's been… a lot."

Tyler stands and for a moment I think he's going to argue it. Instead, he reaches behind the bar and pulls out a leather jacket, holding it out to me.

I hesitate, then let him drape it over my shoulders with quiet authority, as his fingers graze my collarbone.

"Let me get you home," he says quietly.

"Not necessary. I can make my own way," I reply, as I reach for my bag.

He doesn't argue. He studies me for a moment, before nodding.

Tyler simply follows, guiding me down the back staircase.

The bouncer greets us at the exit, tapping knuckles with Tyler as he steps aside and I walk out alone.

"See you around Cass," Tyler mutters softly.

The alley is quiet and when I reach the end, I lean against the cold, hard stone wall and close my eyes, taking a deep breath.

I should go home to sleep. I should go home and close the door on the night and forget about him.

Instead, all I can think about is the way he didn't try to stop me from leaving, he didn't even flinch as I walked away.

My eyes snap open with the unbearable realisation that I'm already in too deep.

I don't want to go. Not yet.

I walk back the way I came, heels echoing loudly in the alley. The back door, still ajar, glowing ahead of me.

He's still there. *Of course he is.*

I watch, transfixed as he swings a leg over his bike, pulls on a helmet and zips his leather jacket with effortless precision.

He looks up and surprise flickers across his face, gone almost as quickly as it appears.

"Changed your mind?" he asks curiously.

"I did."

He studies me for a second longer than necessary before unclipping his helmet.

"Put it on," he commands.

My body succumbs to his demand more quickly than I'd like to admit.

The engine roars to life, vibrating through the narrow alley and the sound sends a thrill straight down my spine. Feeling giddy, I drift towards the bike as if it's magnetic, allowing my fingers to trail over the cool metal, tracing its grooves.

Through his half-open visor, Tyler watches every movement I

make.

"Come on," he says.

He lowers the visor over my face, and the sound of my own breath swells inside the confined space of the helmet, which smells like leather and his woody aftershave.

I climb onto the bike behind him, resting myself on the quilted arch, my arms wrap around his torso, palms flattening against the firm muscles beneath his jacket.

He revs the engine without warning and I jump, tightening my grip.

"Wait, I can't move," he calls back over the roar. "If you pin down my jacket like that, I can't ride."

He lifts the back of his leather jacket so I can slide my arms underneath it, my hands resting against his abs now, only a thin shirt separating us.

I'm grateful to be able to hide behind the helmet.

The engine rumbles between my legs and I swallow hard, each jolt pulls me deeper into the feeling I've been trying to ignore since the moment I saw him.

As the bar fades behind us, the bike surges forward beneath us. The wind cuts against my bare legs but I barely notice it, the whole moment has shrunk to the pull of him. Wrapped in his gravity, pressed close together, I feel the tug of something raw inside me that I know I shouldn't want.

I close my eyes, letting my thoughts bleed into excitement. It almost feels like flying.

Painfully aware of every inch of our bodies that are touching, I realise something that frightens me.

I know this feeling will cost me something, I just don't know what yet.

CHAPTER 9 - FIRE AT MY DOOR

Pulling up outside the entrance to my block, my legs feel like jelly from the adrenaline. Every step away from the bike is an effort to maintain composure as I remove my helmet and reluctantly hand it back to Tyler.

"That was… amazing," I manage, my voice wobbling. I barely stop myself from bouncing on the spot.

His smile reaches his eyes. Something about it makes the careful boundaries I've built crumble.

"Coming up for a drink?" The words tumble out of my mouth.

He studies me for a long, unreadable moment.

"I'll follow you up, Flat 111?"

Nodding, I turn to leave, allowing Tyler to park his bike, but as I do, fear hits.

Did I already tell him my flat number? No. I'm sure I never did, and I don't like how casually he says it.

Before I reach the door my eyes land on a black car idling across the street. I try to brush it off, but I'm sure I've seen it before.

The lift is painfully slow and every noise in the corridor sounds far too loud. My hands are sweaty as I finally slip the keys into the lock on my front door.

Inside, I dump the flutes from earlier into the sink, straighten the cushions and catch a glimpse of myself in the bathroom mirror. I take a deep breath, smoothing my hair, as I steady myself against the counter.

"Get a grip, Cass," I say out loud to myself, like I haven't already lost it more than once today.

My phone buzzes on the side.

Blocked number.

I hit dismiss and quickly text Lola.

'Got a lift home, I'm okay.'

I turn my phone on silent and shove it away before I can overthink about the unease eating away at me.

I make my way back to the kitchen, pulling out two tumblers from the cupboard, when a gentle knock sounds at the door.

"It's open," I call, realising how stupid it was to leave the door on the latch.

Heart hammering, I pour our drinks without looking up.

"Drink?" I ask, turning. "Sorry, no ice."

"No problem."

I settle on the sofa and Tyler follows, sitting on the other end, a small barrier of space separating us. I sip my drink, willing my nerves into submission.

"So…" I let my tongue linger over the word. "Care to explain who you really are?"

I study him closely, searching for cracks, hesitation. Nothing.

"You already know that," he says, arm draped casually along the back of the sofa. The lamp behind him casts shadows that only seem to make him more striking.

"No," I insist. "I want to know who's sitting in my living room. What do you do exactly? How is it that I keep finding you in my life?"

A pang of irrational jealousy coils in my chest. This man could have anyone he wanted.

"I'm a businessman. I own businesses, make friends and

connections, and I am here because you invited me in."

"So, you're here, entertaining my request to come up, when you could be anywhere, with anyone, and instead you choose… me?" My voice carries a challenge.

Tyler tilts his head, resting his hand lightly against his temple. His eyes study me, playful and piercing.

"Because you intrigue me," he says. "You're beautiful… and while I probably shouldn't be here, maybe for your own sanity, I want to be. You've been on my mind all week."

He pauses. "Haven't I been on yours?"

I ignore the question, looking away as Tyler's eyes bore into me. "What business do you do?"

His smile is slow. "Properties. Investments. I own a few things here and there."

Something clicks. I relax fractionally at the familiarity. "I work in property too, not investing, just at a firm."

He nods knowingly. "I know."

Of course he knows.

"How did you know my flat number?" I ask quizzingly.

"Come on Cass, you work in property. You know how easy it is to find an address once you know a name."

No Tyler, that's not how easy it is.

3am blinks on the clock.

Catching my gaze, Tyler pushes himself up from the sofa.

"You've got an important meeting this weekend," he says, "I should go."

How does he know that? How does he know anything?

I swallow as I stand, trying to steady my racing thoughts. "What kind of property do you own, Tyler?"

He steps closer slowly, brushing my hair behind my ear with a tenderness that shouldn't coexist with the panic I'm feeling. His hand cups my chin, his presence suffocating yet, intoxicating.

Leaning into me, I breathe in his woody aftershave. "I own Sparks Developments," he reveals.

To torment me further, he leans in, lips grazing my cheek, too close to my mouth to pretend it's innocent.

"I..." I force myself to breathe. "I don't let people in easily."

My words spill out before I can stop them and I'm slightly embarrassed by my admission.

A memory flashes, hands grabbing my face, a forced kiss, a voice telling me to apologise before...

I push it down.

He nods, his eyes scan my face like he's searching for the answers I'm keeping buried.

Tyler straightens out his shirt and makes his way towards the door.

"Coffee Sunday?" he asks lightly, "across our balconies? Or should we wait for our meeting?" He flashes a grin.

The breath I've been holding explodes out of me.

Oh. My. God.

Before closing the door fully, Tyler pauses and leans back in. "I didn't follow you there," he says quietly. "The night I bumped into you at the restaurant. I didn't plan it, I just didn't waste the chance when it showed up."

"I need you to stop doing that," I say defensively.

Tyler's gaze holds mine. "Doing what?"

"Showing up in my life."

His jaw tightens. "You want answers or reassurance?"

"The truth," I reply.

The hum of the fridge fills the silence.

"I knew who you were before you knew who I was," he sighs.

"Your name crossed my desk a while ago. Property circles aren't as big as people think. When I saw it again on the booking at Chicago's, I noticed."

"Noticed," I reply flatly.

"I recognised you," he corrects.

Cold slides down my spine. "So, you were watching me?"

"I was making sure you got home safe."

"That's not your job."

"No," he agrees. "It wasn't."

I stand, pacing once before turning back to him. "Why has it taken you so long to tell me?"

"I didn't think you'd take it well."

He's right, I wouldn't have.

I press my palm to the back of my neck, grounding myself. "So what is this to you? A game?"

"No Cass," he says firmly. "This isn't a game." His eyes drop momentarily before he continues. "But you are someone I should stay away from."

"Then why don't you?" I whisper.

He looks at me like I should already know the answer.

"Good night, Cass."

The door clicks shut and I rush to lock the door behind him, leaning against the cold wood.

The man I almost told the edge of a confession to, the man whose hands were on me minutes ago...is not only my neighbour, he's our new client.

My mind reverts back to that night on the balcony. Tyler, half-naked, the smashed glass.

I can do nothing but laugh, hot tears stream down my face, unrestrained, as the chaos of the night presses in.

Walking over to close my curtains, the black car I had seen earlier is still idling at the kerb. The headlights are on and someone is inside.

Sleep won't come easy tonight. Not with the ghost of his touch on my skin, or with the truth I almost let slip out burning behind my ribs.

My phone buzzes again.

Blocked number.

My phone screen goes dark, but I can't pull my eyes away.

CHAPTER 10 - LINES ALREADY CROSSED

My phone buzzes before I'm properly awake.

Lola: 'Taken home, I see. I want all the gossip after work.'

My phone buzzes again.

Lola: 'Not happy about you jumping on the back of a motorbike after a night out, but I still do want all the details.'

Normally, I don't work weekends, but preparing for new client meetings is the exception, and when the 'client' is Tyler Sparks, well, my body doesn't get the memo to stay calm.

I spend most of my Saturday morning buried under blueprints and site plans. The restaurant disaster with Liam is now safely tucked away as 'mortifying memories to revisit at 3am', but Tyler, the walking red flag with a jawline crafted by God himself, refuses to leave my mind.

Which is ridiculous. I barely know him and yet…

I shake the thought off and begin shuffling through the floor plans splayed across my desk.

"Cass," Jack beckons from his doorway. "Quick word?"

Great. I grab my notebook and step into his office.

He gestures to the seat opposite him. "Close the door."

That's never a good sign. I sit, bracing for impact.

"The new account we've got coming in," he begins. "Big one, Sparks Developments."

My brain stumbles.

"We need our strongest lead on it," he continues, oblivious to my internal crisis. "And that's you."

"Sparks Developments...the CEO is particular." He pauses.

Don't I already know it.

"He wants someone competent handling staff onboarding and contract executions."

Great, my personal life has just walked into the office without knocking.

"But I was only stepping in to help tomorrow for Carly..." I falter, "I can't take this on full time."

He leans back, scanning me with his eyes.

"You're sharp, organised and you don't let anyone push you around. You're perfect for this."

Funny that, I feel like I'm being pushed around right now.

Jack smiles, "I knew I could count on you."

As I leave his office, my pulse thrums like a trapped bird in a cage.

Back at my desk I stare so hard at my screen I can almost see through it.

My phone buzzes on the desk.

Lola: 'Where are you? I need you.'

Of course she does. Lola never texts like that unless she's planning something reckless, or already has.

I hesitate momentarily before grabbing my bag and heading out.

As the lift doors slide shut, my reflection catches me off guard and I jump back.

I take a deep breath to keep my nerves from fraying further.

Tomorrow I will walk into a professional meeting and pretend

I haven't straddled my new client on his motorbike. I'll act as if I'm not coming undone in places that have been stitched shut.

The lift dings and I step out.

One crisis at a time, Cass.

Lola first, then Tyler and then, if my anxiety feels generous, sleep.

~

I find Lola perched on the arm of my sofa, phone in one hand, the other tugging on the sleeve of her jumper.

"You look dramatic," I comment, slipping off my shoes. "What have you done?"

She laughs too quickly. "Nothing, God Cass. I just need a second opinion."

On what, exactly, isn't clear. She hops up and starts rifling through a shopping bag at the other end of the sofa.

"I bought some clothes and thought you could help," she says.

She holds up a dress, frowns at it and then drops it back into the bag. Her phone lights up, but she doesn't look at it, just flips it face down.

"You okay?" I ask.

"Fine," she says quickly. "Just tired. Overthinking."

"You know I left work early to get home right?" I pause. "It sounded like it was urgent."

I watch her closely, her smile keeps slipping like she needs to keep reminding herself to wear it.

"Lola," I say quietly.

She exhales deeply and slowly, then gestures towards me. "I panicked, alright? I didn't want to call, but my head went somewhere stupid and I just needed grounding."

She finally meets my eyes. "It's nothing, Cass. I swear. Sorry if I worried you."

I let it go.

Not because I believe her. She's never been good at lying when she's worried, but because she's asking me not to push, and I've learned the hard way what happens when I do.

Still, something sits wrong. The way *nothing,* suddenly needs so much explaining.

If I ask the questions I really want to ask, she'll either shut down or lie better and I don't have the energy for either. So, I nod, offer my opinions on the clothes and make the right noises.

Whatever's bothering her, she'll tell me when she's ready.

CHAPTER 11 - THE MAN BEHIND THE CURTAIN

Dragging myself out of bed and into the shower, I force myself into my familiar morning routine.

I put on my pale blue two-piece suit with my white chiffon blouse that just hints at cleavage, paired with my Valentino heels. For good measure, I've painted my nails red to match my lipstick.

All to look professional. Well, that's at least what I tell myself until I look in the mirror. I'm dressing for him.

My eyes settle on the leather jacket he lent me. His scent rises immediately, warm, woody and intoxicating, tugging at last night's memories.

My gaze drifts to the coffee table, my ID and bank card sit there innocently.

Impossible. They weren't there before. I know that because I tore this place apart looking and reported them missing.

I reach for them with a shaking hand, half expecting them to disappear once more. I push my thoughts aside. I don't have time to spiral right now.

I force a breath, lock the door behind me and grip my keys like a weapon.

~

I park in the multistorey and decide last minute to bring Tyler's leather jacket with me. My phone buzzes as I lock the car.

Blocked caller. Again.

A hollow, twisting ache fills my stomach. That's the third time this morning. I silence it and hurry down to meet Rachael. I hand her the coffee I grabbed for her as she taps away on her phone.

"Sorry, doll, there's a bit of an emergency at home. Hubby's useless," she says with a gentle smile.

Rachael launches into HR chatter as we walk briskly toward the high-rise development and I try not to fall apart.

"For 150 units, we'll need at least five people. Have you got CVs ready?"

"They're on the shared drive," I reply, trying to concentrate.

Rachael was here to help me put together some HR policies and finalise ATR forms so we can begin recruiting staff before residents start moving in.

My phone buzzes again.

Blocked Caller.

The vibration rattles through my palm like a warning. I shove the phone into my coat pocket.

Rachael's phone buzzes too. "Sorry, doll. I really need to take this. "Go ahead, I'll catch up."

A smartly dressed blonde greets me.

"Good morning, you must be Miss Palazzo?"

"That's right," I say, smiling. "My colleague and I are here to meet Mr Sparks at 8am."

She guides me into a glass meeting room, quickly disappearing back to her post. I check the time: **07:50**.

"Cass."

I freeze.

Tyler stands in the doorway, holding it open with his foot. Dressed immaculately, but somehow a little softer than he looked the other night. His tie isn't done yet and his hair is still slightly damp.

"I didn't know you were coming down now," I say, too rehearsed.

"I saw you walking in from my office," a glint passes through his eyes.

"Thought I'd come greet you. It's a big day. Let's grab a coffee."

His gentleness throws me more off balance than any smirk of his ever has.

I nod, adjusting my bag over my shoulder, as I follow him out of the meeting room and down the corridor.

We stand in silence until the coffee machine whirrs to life.

"Did you sleep the other night?" He asks softly.

Too simple a question considering the chaos of our last encounter.

I swallow. "Eventually."

Tyler's hands are in his pockets, watching the coffee drip into the mug, as if he's choosing his next words carefully. "You seemed… lighter on Friday."

A soft exhale escapes me. "I don't feel very light today."

Another buzz. I look down.

Blocked Caller.

He glances at me and then his eyes warm in a way that makes my chest tighten unexpectedly.

"You don't have to pretend with me," he murmurs.

He turns to face me fully, and for the first time since I've met him, there is no arrogance or playful smirk that follows.

"Cass…I enjoy getting to know you. Not just the version of you who hides behind comebacks. I like…" his throat flexes as he swallows. "I like the quiet parts too."

"I…" my voice trails off as he steps close enough that his jacket brushes my sleeve.

"I just want to understand you," his voice is barely above a whisper. "People think they know where I come from, but they don't, not really."

A flicker of thought crosses his features, disappearing as fast as it came.

I'm not used to moments like this, or to men who offer softness instead of taking advantage of it.

I meet his gaze.

"If you want me to understand you…" I swallow, "Then tell me something real. What's your biggest regret?"

"You don't start small, do you?" he says with a faint smile. He looks down at the floor, thumb rubbing the edge of his cuff.

"When I was fourteen, I didn't show up to my sister's school performance. I promised her I'd be there. She was playing the star in the Nativity, but I was working for my father that night instead."

His face hardens. "She never asked me to come to anything again."

My chest aches, but I don't say anything.

He hesitates, a vulnerability so fleeting I almost miss it, and reaches for his wallet. He slides a photo free and offers it to me without a word.

I take it carefully, the photo is worn around edges. A little girl stands on a school stage beneath tinsel and paper snowflakes, wearing a foil halo and a gold dress that's slightly too big for her. Tyler's eyes don't look away.

"When I was in my twenties, a man hurt someone I cared

about. I let him walk away because my father told me to stand down. I've never forgotten his face."

The room feels heavier; his words carry weight, and I'm not quite sure where to place them. I'd known Tyler carried something dark, but hearing it…it made him real in a way that terrifies me.

It wasn't the danger around him that scared me, it was how much I suddenly wanted to stand between him and the people who had hurt him.

"What about you?" he asks softly. "Your biggest regret?"

My palms go cold.

The memory crashes into me, the last time *he* was near, the blood, the cold tiles. My scar burns at the thought.

"I…" but nothing more comes out.

Tyler doesn't press me to answer.

The coffee machine beeps to signal it's finished, breaking the moment. Tyler glances at his watch and straightens.

"I'll walk you to the meeting room and let you go in alone so you don't feel…compromised."

A laugh bursts out of me, surprising us both.

As we reach the door to the meeting room, I stop and turn to him. Tyler adjusts my collar without thinking, smoothing the fabric with surprising care, and for a moment, the world goes quiet around us.

I step back, I need to.

"See you inside, Mr Sparks."

His expression shifts, a corner of a smile he tries to hide, follows me all the way through the door.

Settling at the desk, Rachael breezes in moments later. "Hun, I have to dash. Lily broke her arm; I need to meet her at the hospital."

She places her bag on the table. "The client today? Handsome, very wealthy. Owns buildings, bars, you name it. Smart. Knows what he wants. If I weren't happily married, I'd jump on that horse..." she laughs, shaking her head.

A deep voice cuts through my thoughts. "Sorry I'm late. Missed the joke, I see."

Glancing at Rachael, her cheeks flush pink. Did he hear us?

I rise to my feet, my professional mask firmly in place. "Mr Sparks, pleasure to meet you," I say brightly.

"Mr Sparks, lovely to see you. Sorry, I have to cut this short, family emergency," she blurts, clearing her throat. "Miss Palazzo will be able to feedback to me about anything she needs my assistance with." She glances back at me with a curt nod.

"Thank you both, a pleasure again Mr Sparks. Cass, I'll give you a call later once I get back to a laptop."

Grabbing her bag, she hurriedly leaves the room.

Neither Tyler nor I move an inch until the door clicks shut.

I clear my throat and pull out my chair. He follows, sitting across from me.

He smirks. "No need for formalities at work, Cass. Call me Tyler."

I observe Tyler from the corner of my eye. Taking a sip of water, his stance is confident. Muscular legs wide apart, he sits with his back straight against the chair. The suit is too well-fitted to be cheap; it has been made to measure.

He loosens his tie, undoing the top button of his shirt and a tattoo peeks out.

I want to crawl into a hole and stay there until I cool down.

"I've got candidates for your positions," I say, tucking a loose strand of hair behind my ear. Tyler rises, moving beside me, his scent envelops me.

I type in my password and his face fills my entire screen.

Fuck.

I'd forgotten to close my browser during another late-night investigative session.

I slam the laptop screen down and squeeze my eyes shut. Kill me now.

When I open one eye, Tyler is smirking, hands clasped behind his head.

A trace of amusement dances across his face. "Still here," he teases.

Reaching forward, Tyler prizes open my laptop and his face flashes up on the screen again.

"I knew you were going to fall for me, but I didn't think it would be in a stalker kind of way."

My body tenses at the word.

I swat his hand away, nervous laughter spilling from me. "I'm not great with technology," I admit. "I wanted to thank you, actually."

"For… what?" He tilts his head, eyes burning.

"Dropping me home. Lucky for me, a picture popped up from Sparks rooftop last night when I was on Facebook. Couldn't sleep after," I lie.

I narrow my eyes at him. "Your bar," I correct.

"If I had my way, you wouldn't have gotten any sleep at all," his voice teasing.

"I've shortlisted three candidates already," I say quickly, forcing myself back onto safer ground.

"Two for front of house, strong CV's, clean references, both with experience in high-end property portfolios."

Tyler's expression sharpens.

"And the last?" he asks, casually.

"I'm meeting him tomorrow," I reply. "Recruiter says he's solid, but I want to hear it from him myself."

"Good," Tyler replies. "I don't hire on paper."

Tyler flicks his gaze to the open tabs for half a second, then back to me.

"I have two potentials for operations. One's a steady pair of hands, the other more strategic, but I think I'd want you in the interview for that one."

Tyler leans back in his chair, his fingers steepled.

"I can arrange first-stage interviews by the end of the week," I add, heart still thudding. "I've already aligned the salaries to the market rate and asked for notice periods and current packages upfront so nobody wastes your time."

"Efficient," he hums. "Dangerous combination on you." He pauses momentarily.

"What are you doing after our meeting Cass?" he asks without flinching.

"You… I mean, work. For you. Finding candidates."

He throws back his head and laughs. A rich, chesty sound that makes the room shrink.

"Keep talking like that, and you won't be leaving here at all."

He taps his fingers on the desk. "Let's save this meeting for somewhere without watchful eyes."

He stands first and I follow, Tyler towers over me even though I'm 5'8" in heels, leaving me feeling small beside him.

"Lunch?" he asks. "2:30 at Zagara's, it's more private. We can continue our discussion," he pauses. "I have a meeting shortly. I'll be finished by then."

"Great," I manage, trying to steady myself.

He presses the red buzzer. "Alexandra, clear my schedule after 2pm. Book a table for two at Zagara's, 2:30 this afternoon, Important business proposition."

He lifts my hand to his lips and plants a gentle kiss. "Don't be late Cass, I just cleared my schedule for you."

Just before Tyler leaves the room, he stops in the door frame, long enough that my eyes flit up to look at him.

I hear my phone buzz on the coffee table.

"Just so you know," Tyler pauses, "I had already decided I wanted you on my team. I just didn't expect to want you any other way."

I sit on the chair, stunned, the echo of his presence lingering long after he strides out of the room.

Reaching for my phone, the screen lights up.

Blocked Caller.

Tyler didn't just stumble into my life, he chose to.

CHAPTER 12 - DANCING WITH THE DEVIL

Unable to focus on work since that morning meeting, I text Rachael to check on her daughter, casually mentioning that the business meeting had been extended. If only she knew.

My phone flashes: 2:25 pm.

Zagara's is quiet, except for a man alone in a suit nursing a beer at the bar.

My breath hitches when my eyes fall on Tyler. Pausing, I take in the furrow of his brow, the distracted rub at his stubble and his slightly dishevelled hair. Even sitting alone, he commands the room.

When he looks up and notices me, his frown relaxes into that familiar magnetic smile, and he steps out of the booth to greet me.

In the last twenty-four hours, I've broken more HR policies than I care to admit, starting with number two: no personal relationships with employees, clients, or residents. My stomach clenches at the thought.

"Tyler," I say softly.

"Cass," he smiles, casually unbuttoning his suit jacket.

I slide out of my blazer, folding it neatly on the chair beside me. "This is yours," I say, placing his leather jacket across the table.

"Thank you," he murmurs. "I took the liberty of ordering us drinks. I know it's early, so I went for virgin," he sits, eyes flicking to mine with that unreadable expression that makes me giddy.

I grab the drinks menu, flipping straight to the cocktail section. "That's a shame."

Tyler's eyebrows lift, eyes suddenly aflame. He opens his mouth to reply, but the waiter interrupts with our drinks.

"Could I also order a Sex on the Beach, please?" I ask, glancing at him. His eyes narrow, intrigued.

"Two, please," Tyler adds before the waiter shuffles away.

Finally, alone, I lean forward.

"Look, Tyler... had I known before Friday that you were the client I was meeting today, things wouldn't have played out the same. I've worked hard to get here, and while I'm flattered... I pride myself on my work."

He tilts his head, voice low. "And I knew someone as stubborn as you wouldn't sit down with me for longer than five minutes unless you had to."

"That's not true," I interject too quickly, the flush creeping up my neck. "Maybe it is, but...."

Tyler leans back, scanning the empty restaurant.

"You're..." I waver, searching for words. "Very intriguing."

His gaze snaps back to me, sharp and assessing.

Trying to shake off the nerves clawing at my chest, I suggest a distraction.

"Let's play a game," my eyes tease as I lay my hand flat on the table. "Do you have a coin?"

He reaches into his pocket and produces a £1 coin, dropping it into my palm.

"Heads, I ask a question. Tails, you get to."

He leans forward, sleeves rolled up, tanned skin catching the light, his thumbs pressing near his lips.

"Deal," he says, voice low. "Let's keep it light this time, shall we?"

I flip the coin. Heads. Relief floods me. "How old are you... Mr Sparks?"

He chuckles, folding his arms. "Thirty-one."

Hard to believe there are seven years between us. No wonder his presence is so intimidating, making every man I've dated feel juvenile.

Flipping the coin, it lands on heads again.

"You're setting me up," his eyes glitter with amusement.

"Don't be a sore loser..." I pause, flicking a glance at his mouth, imagining it on mine. "Had any dreams about me?"

He quirks an eyebrow. "Seriously?"

"Did I stutter?" I sip my drink, trying to sound casual, all the while that balcony memory stabs through me. Tyler watches me as if he can see right into the heat behind my eyes.

I flip the coin.

Tails. He leans forward, taking a sip of his drink. "Do you always play this hard to get, or are you simply arrogant?"

I snort. "Presumptuous. Just because I haven't dropped my panties and spread-eagled for you when you say please, doesn't make me arrogant. Maybe you're too used to getting your own way."

"Great visualisation," he mutters, smirking.

"Look," Tyler says, his voice low. "There's a reason I don't let people get close either."

He hesitates, fingers tapping once against his thigh.

"It's not because I'm cold. It's because I learnt the hard way that the people you think you can trust..." He exhales sharply. "Can sell you out without a second thought."

I stay still, afraid to interrupt.

"My father was…" he stops, jaw flexing, "a real piece of work. Growing up, he'd disappear for days. Sometimes weeks, and when he was actually around, he made sure we knew we weren't his priority."

A bitter smile curves at his mouth.

"He was into shady deals. The kind of stuff you don't talk about unless you want trouble knocking on your door at three in the morning."

I fidget slightly in my seat.

"Eventually, he racked up a debt with the wrong people," Tyler continues quietly. "And guess who he offered up?"

A heavy silence settles in the air.

"Me," he says. "I became the bargaining chip he couldn't live without."

I inhale sharply, but Tyler keeps going, his voice steady in that way people get when their story has lived inside them for so long.

"So, for a few years, I worked it off. Took every failing bar, club, or absolute shit hole they shoved in front of me and turned it around. Made it profitable. Kept my head down."

He pauses again briefly. "It was survival and a whole lot of pretending I wasn't angry at the world."

A heavy, exhausted sigh pushes out of him.

I want to reach for him, to say something that might lighten the load, but the words stick in my throat, glued there by shock. All I can do is breathe through the sudden sting in my eyes and hope he doesn't mistake my silence for judgment, rather than the heartbreak it truly is.

"Tyler…" I whisper.

"You weren't supposed to hear all that," he mutters quickly. "It just slipped out."

"Because it's the truth," I say gently, "And you've been carrying it alone for a long time."

That's a feeling I'm friends with all too well.

He looks away, like my kindness physically hurts him.

Without missing a beat, Tyler flips the coin. Tails again.

"Will you let me take you on a proper date?"

Alcohol and desire make my thoughts spin. My restraint is razor-thin when it comes to Tyler Sparks.

"No."

"Why not?" he questions.

"Because I'm not allowed to date clients or anyone I work with. Policy."

He leans in, his expression sharpening. "So quit," he teases. "Come work for me."

I shrug, laughing nervously. "Sure, when do I start?"

"I'm serious," he says, the lines around his eyes deepening, filled with longing.

"I know your portfolio, Cass. You're talented, only twenty-four, more successful than people ten years older. You're attractive and sharp-tongued…" His gaze flickers to my lips.

My head spins. I wave over the waiter, needing something solid in my hands.

Running his hands through his hair, he tenses and rests one arm on the back of the sofa seat.

"Think about it."

By 6:30pm, my reflection in the bathroom mirror is almost unrecognisable. Mascara crumbling and my lipstick patchy.

I've learnt more about Tyler over dinner tonight than in all our previous encounters combined. Piece by piece, he allowed parts of himself to slip through the cracks, revealing not the polished version he presents to the world, but the man beneath.

The history between him and his sister is messy, full of things neither of them seem ready to unpack. Yet, when he mentioned her son, *"my sister's kid… don't ask, it's complicated"*, there was a warmth in his voice. Something protective. He might pretend otherwise, but he's fond of that little boy.

He even talked about his father. A man who disappeared. A man who made promises he never kept.

As he spoke, the sharpness in him eased and the less he seemed like the arrogant arse who seems to enjoy winding me up. He's just someone human, flawed…someone who's trying.

Tonight, I've seen a side of Tyler I didn't expect, one that is gradually unfolding me, allowing me to open up again without needing complete control over everything.

My phone buzzes and breaks me out of my thoughts.

A text from Rachael.

'Hey doll, glad all is well. Catch up tomorrow?'

I tuck my phone away, heart still pounding from the evening.

Walking back to the table, Tyler stands to greet me.

"The bill's paid. Let me walk you out."

"You shouldn't have," I say quietly, my voice weak.

His hand finds the small of my back as we step into the warm evening. The sunset paints the city in flames and the breeze teases the thin silk of my blouse. I feel him glance down and I'm incredibly thankful for my last-minute change of lingerie this morning.

He wraps an arm around my waist, pulling me closer in an embrace that feels comfortable.

"No lover waiting at home tonight?" I joke, breathless.

"Let's get you home." He stops near a black cab, eyes fixed on mine, unwavering.

I nod and step into the cab, followed closely by Tyler.

The journey home is charged. The air is heavy with unspoken

words and a few stolen looks that burn hotter than anything we spoke about over dinner.

When we pull up outside my building, relief mingles with anticipation. I inhale deeply, letting the evening air steady me before I walk inside.

As we enter the lobby, the soft lighting and the faint scent of Tyler's aftershave drifting past my shoulder pulls me sharply back into myself, and instinctively, my back presses against the wall.

He steps in front of me, close enough that his breath warms my cheek.

Our eyes meet, and it feels like the entire day is pressed between us, every question, each truth, all the boundaries we blurred.

His gaze drops to my mouth and stays there. His hand brushes my hair back gently behind my shoulder, with knuckles grazing my skin, before his hand settles at the back of my neck. His hand lifts carefully, like he's giving me time to pull away.

I should stop this; I should remember what wanting someone has cost me before…but he's so close, my skin aches for contact.

Unable to deny him any longer, I taste his mouth on mine before I feel it.

My lips find his first, almost pleading, before the kiss deepens into something I can't control. I melt into him, pressing closer, as his tongue slides against mine and his stubble grazes my lips.

His hand wraps hard around my waist, pulling me flush against him. I match his urgency, his hunger. My body reacts to his as though it has been waiting since long before I ever admitted I wanted him.

One hand slides to the back of my head, possessive in the gentlest way, while the other drifts lower under my blouse, fingers brushing the edge of my bra.

Then, his thumb sweeps over the scar at the base of my skull.

My ears block out all noise and a cold rush sweeps through me like I've been punched.

Not here. Not now. He doesn't know.

"Don't move," he whispers against my lips, unaware of my inner turmoil.

Too late. I'm already dragged back into the memory of the cold floor and a hand that wasn't gentle, forcing my head down until I apologised.

No. Stop. Not now.

I pull myself out of the kiss, my breathing erratic.

Tyler's face shifts instantly, confusion flickering across his features.

I pull myself upright, smoothing my blouse.

"Thank you for tonight, Tyler," my voice sharper than I intend. "I'll… send over the brief tomorrow."

I see the way his expression shifts, his eyebrows furrow as he runs his hand through his hair.

The lift pings and I step inside, giving him a small nod.

He doesn't move or smile, he just stands there, impossibly handsome even with my lipstick smudged across his mouth, and when the doors slide shut between us, I steady myself against the cold lift wall.

I slip into my flat, kick my heels off and lean against my locked door trying to catch my breath.

My phone buzzes with a text.

Unknown Number.

My pulse picks up and then slows as I realise who it's from.

"Goodnight Miss Palazzo. Thank you for an interesting evening."

A second buzz.

"Oh, please tell Rachael not to bet on any horses, especially not this one. He doesn't go for married women."

A laugh bursts out of me, sudden and breathless.

He heard everything.

I type a reply with trembling fingers.

"Good night, Mr Sparks."

I place my phone on charge, heart still racing.

Tyler was bleeding into places I'd kept sealed for years and my brain hasn't caught up with the fact that I didn't hate it… I just didn't trust it either.

CHAPTER 13 - UNKNOWN NUMBER

The past two days have blurred into a haze of Teams calls, checklists, and towering piles of paperwork. My pen taps an erratic rhythm against my desk.

Taking on two new clients this week meant I hadn't left the office before 9pm once, and honestly, it was a welcome distraction from thoughts of Tyler. From what almost happened...from what did happen.

My phone blinks 8pm, and my stomach reminds me of its dissatisfaction. Dinner with Lola is booked for 8:30pm, and I felt a rush of relief knowing she had chosen the small Italian trattoria down the road from my office. Our favourite spot. A place we visited at least twice a month, a ritual of warmth and familiarity.

Lola had been pestering me since our night out for a catch up and I feel bad about ignoring her.

The reason was both simple and complicated all at once. She would pry about the weekend. About Tyler and I wasn't ready yet. Things spiralled faster than I could control the other night and I need to keep reminding myself why my walls are up in the first place.

I reach for the back of my neck, fingers grazing the scar there and a shiver runs through me. A reminder. I squeeze my eyes shut.

Pushing open the trattoria's door, I'm immediately greeted by the familiar warmth and the comforting aroma of the wood-fired pizza oven.

There she is, Lola, sitting with her back to me at a table by the bar. Memories wash over me like waves; the aroma of cannoli, the tang of fresh tomato sauce. Italy. Holidays spent with my father's family. I had been fluent in Italian as a child, but years without practice had dulled my tongue. Still, I understood enough to be swept away by nostalgia.

Leaning down, I wrap my arms around Lola, squeezing tightly and pressing a kiss to her cheek.

"Cass! Good God, you look amazing. I've missed you so much." Her grin stretches ear to ear as she returns my hug, "Aperol Spritz?"

"Uh, duh. That's the only reason I came," I say with mock exasperation, and we both laugh.

A young waiter appears, dimples flashing as he greets us.

He leaves with our drink order and Lola leans forward. "I know you've been distant this week. Work stress?"

I sigh. "You know me too well..."

"Hmm," she says knowingly. "Or perhaps you've got some hottie from the bar the other night locked up somewhere and you're keeping him a secret?"

"Oh, you have no idea," I exaggerate, cupping my hands dramatically over my mouth. "The only reason I escaped our tiresome bed frolicking is because I left him tied to the headboard in fluffy handcuffs. Shit...I forgot to leave him water!"

Lola slaps my arm, laughing so hard I feel the warmth of her joy in my chest.

When the waiter returns with menus and takes our order, I straighten, seriousness creeping back in.

"Lola, I need to talk to you."

Rolling her eyes, she groans, "God, Cass, can't we eat first?"

"I need to know what happened a couple of weeks ago? You can talk to me, you know that, right?"

She drops her elbows onto the table, eyes hardening before softening again, like she's debating how much to admit.

"I know," she said slowly. "James forbade me from telling anyone, especially you."

James forbade?

My heartbeat quickens.

"You know how close we are," she continues. "Remember when I said I'd been seeing James for a while now?"

I nod.

She picks at the napkin, tearing it into thin strips.

"Remember Spotty Shane? The Tinder date disaster? Well..." she swallows. "I told him we weren't compatible. I thought he took it well, but then he suggested one last drink. After that... everything went blurry."

Her voice trembles as tears gather in her eyes. I reach for her hand and she grips mine like she's drowning.

"He pinned my arm so hard I thought it would break. Then I saw James. He was carrying me. That's where I woke up."

The bitter taste of bile rises up my throat and I struggle to swallow it back down.

"Lola, why didn't you tell me?"

She hugs me, patting my shoulder, but something about it feels rehearsed, like she's trying to comfort herself rather than me.

"James made sure I was safe. That's all I know. He said it was handled."

Handled how?

She freezes.

For a moment, her mouth opens as if she's about to tell

me everything, the real truth she's hiding behind the polished version.

"Cass... there's something I didn't..."

The waiter arrives with our food and she snaps shut instantly. Her entire face resets.

My suspicion flares so intensely, I feel it in my throat.

After he leaves, she pushes her plate aside untouched.

"Cass... James isn't the one to worry about," she says quietly. "One of the guys... he's messed up. He's covered in tattoos. Personal legacy or some shit."

My phone is in my hand before I really think about it as Tyler's name flickers through my mind uninvited.

This isn't his problem and I'm not about to make it one, so I slide my phone back into my bag and squeeze Lola's hand instead.

"Just be careful," I whisper. "I just hope you know what you're doing."

She smiles. "James makes me happy."

I want to believe her, I really do. "Don't get caught up in his shit," I murmur.

She sticks her tongue out. "Anyway. Are you going to tell me what *you* got up to this weekend?"

I lean back, lips pressed together.

"Urgh, you bore."

I signal the waiter for the bill, determined to dodge her questions about my weekend.

"Also," she adds, leaning in over the table, "I have someone lined up for you. A date, someone I actually think you'd really like."

"I'm not really interested," I reply.

Lola blinks. "What?"

"I think I just need a break from dating," I lie.

"Come on, it only has to be one drink, one hour –"

"I'm just... not in the mood," I say, too quickly.

Lola's gaze lingers on my face. "Right..."

My phone buzzes and I reach for my bag, avoiding her eyes.

She tilts her head. "This wouldn't happen to have anything to do with the mystery man you've been weirdly quiet about lately, would it?"

"There is no mystery man," I reply defensively.

Lola smiles slowly, like she's caught scent of my lie. "If you say so."

I tap my phone and a text pops up on the screen.

'When can I see you again?'

Tyler.

Glancing up, I see Lola already buried in her phone.

'As soon as the non-fraternization policy has been abolished.' I type, heart hammering.

Tyler: 'Sparks Developments doesn't have policies that ruin all the fun.' His reply comes almost immediately.

'Ah, what a shame that mine does...' I tap out.

As we step out of the restaurant into the cool evening air, Lola links my arm and pulls me in close.

"So," she says, "I'm going away."

There it is, no warning, dropped into conversation like an afterthought.

I stiffen. "Away where?"

She shrugs. "Just...away. Somewhere with sun. I need a break."

"A break from what?" I ask, sharper than I mean to.

Her smile remains steady, but something in her eyes shifts.

"From you," she teases. "You're exhausting."

"Charming."

"I try." Her grip on my arm tightens as we continue walking down the road.

"Who are you going with?" I ask suspiciously.

"James," she says too easily.

"Since when?"

She tilts her head, studying me. "Does it matter?"

"Yes," I insist, "because it's you."

She sighs, easing her grip on me. "Cass, it's nothing. He's nice, looks after me and I enjoy spending time with him. Why so many questions anyway?"

"Why now?" I ask, my voice barely more than a whisper.

She opens her mouth, then closes it. The pause is brief but unmistakable.

"Because I want to," she says with a sigh.

I watch her closely, I can tell that my interrogation is annoying her, but she knows me too well to think I'll just swallow the first answer she gives. She keeps her gaze focused straight ahead, refusing to give me anything else.

"You're being weird Lo."

She smiles at me, properly this time, meeting my eyes.

"Am I?" she says softly. "Or are you just not used to knowing everything?"

The words sting more than they should.

"You know the parts of me I let you see," she says.

I pull my arm away.

"That's not fair."

"Neither is this face," she points out. "You've been wound tight for weeks."

"Well, you disappearing doesn't help. You always seem to be

busy at the moment," I huff quietly.

"I just need some space, Cass." Her shoulders rise and fall once.

Lola checks her phone, the screen lighting her face. Her eyes flit across the screen before she locks it again and slips it back into her pocket.

"I should go," she exhales. "I've got things to do."

She presses a kiss to my cheek and flags down a cab.

"Don't get into trouble while I'm gone," her eyes scan my face, sharp with warning. "I mean it. Be careful."

She slips into the cab and it pulls away before I can say anything else, before I get the entire truth out of her. The taillights vanish down the road, swallowed by traffic, and I'm left standing alone on the pavement, feeling strangely lost.

From you. You're exhausting.

The words replay whether I want them to or not.

I know Lola, and I know she didn't mean it. It sounded more like deflection than anything else, but from what?

Lola would usually tell me everything, inside out and back to front, without missing a single detail.

I drag in a breath, but it doesn't reach where I need it to.

I've spent years being the one who notices the cracks forming beneath her feet, the one bracing for the fall she insists won't come. I tell myself I'm protecting her, but standing here, alone, makes me wonder how much of that protection is really just fear. Fear that she won't need me to catch her at all.

Unfairly, I suppose I'd used Lola as my safety net after everything happened with my ex. Focusing on her gave the perfect distraction.

Maybe she's right, maybe it is nothing, and I'm just not used to her pulling away from me.

At least I try to convince myself that's what it is.

CHAPTER 14 - THE LINES WE CROSS

"It's important to make your audience feel engaged. If you can hold a conversation with them, fantastic, but remember, what's your selling point? What's your pull?"

I glance at my watch. 2:30 pm. My eyelids feel as if they are weighted down with lead.

Why, oh why, does the company think Friday afternoons were a brilliant time for motivational speakers?

Around the room, everyone looks equally exhausted; pens twirl, notebooks are doodled in, eyes glazed over.

"Right, folks," the facilitator chirps. "Five-minute break, then a guest speaker for the last half-hour."

I head straight for the back of the room, pour myself a coffee, and silently pray that the next thirty minutes pass without incident or, failing that, that I can somehow slip under the table unnoticed.

A gentle nudge to my side makes me jump. "Hey, doll."

Rachael, who is carrying her own coffee like a lifeline, grins at me. "Struggling to stay awake too?"

I suppress a laugh. Rachael was a breath of fresh air in this fossilised office.

I drag my lips into a sad pout. "You have no idea. How's your little one doing?"

She grimaces playfully. "A pink cast, some medicine…broken

bone. But she'll survive. Probably."

I nudge her gently and she laughs.

The room falls silent as we take our seats and I seize the opportunity to fire off a few emails from my phone while we wait.

"Thank you all for having me this afternoon," says a voice I know far too well. I look up.

Tyler. Standing at the front. The guest speaker.

I nearly choke on my coffee.

"I won't bore you," he says as the HR ladies giggle like schoolgirls. "I know most of you want to be out the door by 3:30 for a Friday drink..."

The room fills with the harmonious laughs of all the ladies from HR, most of whom are suddenly twirling their hair and leaning forward full of energy.

"My name is Tyler Sparks, the CEO of Sparks Developments."

It takes a lot for me to stop myself from rolling my eyes. I take another sip of my coffee and set my mug down, letting my eyes sweep over his attire.

"As someone who owes their success to hard work and dedication, I want a show of hands of those who..."

My mind shuts down. All I can see is that kiss, the brush of his thumb along my cheek. The taste of him. My coffee gradually warms, becoming utterly irrelevant.

"And you?" his voice cuts through my brain fog.

Everyone's staring at me. Oh, brilliant. I blink. "Sorry... could you repeat the question?"

Wrinkling my nose in embarrassment, I wish the ground would swallow me up.

A slow grin tugs at the corner of his mouth. "I asked for a show of hands from anyone who thinks engagement through conversation is the most effective way of reeling someone in."

I straighten in my chair. "Well... essentially, there must be initial attraction to the item or service. Otherwise, you're just... talking to a brick wall."

His arms are crossed, eyes glinting with devilish amusement, like he's enjoying every second of this.

"Put it this way, if you're trying to sell meat to a vegetarian, no matter how charming your pitch, they're not suddenly going to gnaw on a T-bone out of politeness."

"Good," he says, eyes steady on mine. "Conversation only works if you know your audience. Once you do, they'll start wanting more, so long as you keep it engaging."

His eyes dip to my lips, just for a moment, like he's remembering.

"It's why questions like this or that and heads or tails work so well," he says softly. "Because the moment they engage, they're showing interest."

My stomach does a somersault. "You're talking about marketing?"

"I'm talking about you."

Tyler doesn't break eye contact.

Then he turns, casually, addressing the room as if he's just realised he needs to be clearer. "I mean your audience," he says smoothly. "The customer, the person on the other end of the conversation."

His gaze flicks back to me, deliberately. "Once you understand what they respond to," he adds in a low voice, "their weak spots, likes and dislikes... They'll answer without thinking."

His eyes linger on me for a moment longer before he turns away.

I slump in my chair, finally taking a breath, dreaming of a hot bath and perhaps a quiet cry into my wine glass.

The meeting ends, and I tiptoe toward the door, praying to

avoid further embarrassment. Clare, petite and perfect-toothed, is keeping Tyler distracted with marketing banter, God bless her.

I finally make it back to my desk, ready to lock myself away in Excel spreadsheets when my laptop pings. Cat, another of our directors, wants to see me.

If she summons you, it wasn't for small talk.

I pack my things, trying to ignore the dread twisting in my belly, and head straight to her office.

Knocking lightly, I hear Cat laugh from behind the door and I tense without meaning to.

"Come in."

I open the door and there he is, Tyler, in all his three-piece glory.

Attempting a casual hello, my right foot betrays me.

In four-inch stilettos with heels thinner than a toothpick, I go down like a sack of potatoes. The contents of my bag stage a rebellion across the cream carpet; lipstick, chewing gum, tampon… and a condom.

On show for both Cat and Tyler to see, I gather the items in haste, as I pull myself up as graciously as I can.

Beads of sweat form at the back of my neck, my bun has gone rogue and my pinky toe hangs precariously from my shoe like it has its own social life.

Cat's eyes widen as she jumps up from her chair. Tyler smirks, hand strategically placed to hide his amusement, but he saw it.

Oh, he saw it.

"I was just telling Mr. Sparks that, as a senior regional manager, it was important he meet you," Cat says, pausing briefly, before settling back in her chair.

I open my mouth. Nothing.

The condom incident replaying in my head in slow motion.

"Please… sit, Cass," Cat gestures next to Tyler.

"You've worked hard, and unless you're after my job, this is a good opportunity to broaden your experience," she continues with a stiff laugh.

Am I getting fired?

"Mr. Sparks has decided to invest here. It's been in the pipeline for a few months…so you'll intern at Sparks as a senior manager for the next two months. Learn everything. Bring it back. Implement changes."

I blink. "I… but my clients?"

"Rachael has it covered," Cat says breezily. "You'll survive."

Tyler stands, extending a hand towards me. My pulse launches into orbit. The electric jolt through my arm feels suspiciously like the one from our last encounter.

"Welcome to Sparks, Cass," he says. "Exciting months ahead."

If I survive this, I'm never leaving my flat again.

CHAPTER 15 - INTO THE WEB

Having spent the entire weekend barricaded in my flat, trying to rationalise the events of Friday and erase all memory of the condom flying out of my bag, it's nothing short of a miracle that I've managed to drag myself out of bed for 7 a.m. on a Monday.

Tapping the steering wheel to the beat of *Too Sweet* by Hozier, I try to suppress the wave of wariness I've been burying all weekend. No such luck. It's still there, humming through my chest like an alarm.

Pulling into the car park behind Sparks Developments, I'm over an hour and a half early. I kill the engine, the hum fading into an almost mocking silence.

A sudden rap at the window freezes me in place.

Blinking, I look up from my phone and my eyes land on a pair of muscular legs in shorts, his arms resting on the handles of a bike. He lowers himself into view and a face appears; dark brown eyes framed by thick lashes, jet-black hair, and a beard so perfect it looks like it was sculpted with surgical precision.

"First day? I don't recognise you," he says, a crooked grin tugging at his lips.

"Is it that obvious?" my voice cracks.

He glances at the empty car park. "I'm Luke," he extends his hand out to me.

"Cass," his grip is firm.

"First day, huh? There's a good coffee shop just down the main road," he says, glancing at his watch. "Ah, I'm going to be late. Great meeting you, early bird," he runs a hand through his dishevelled hair. "See you around."

He smiles like he's rehearsed doing it a thousand times, a smile you don't see until it's too late. My early morning nerves clip back even further.

I watch him climb the stairs, calves flexing with every step.

Cycling. I roll my eyes. People who ride bikes for fitness are unbearable.

Patting down my coat, I head towards the overly grand entrance. Whitewashed walls rise high, crystal chandeliers hang low, and the space is so vast it echoes my own nervous footsteps. To my right, two lifts are tucked behind a large desk where a brown-haired woman sits, elegantly poised behind thick-rimmed glasses.

"Good morning, I'm Cass. First day at Sparks Developments."

"Good morning, Cass," she smiles warmly, her slightly crooked teeth peeking out.

"I'm Charlie, I work here 7 a.m. to 7 p.m, Monday through Friday."

She hands me a freshly printed pass. "Floor 11. Lift's over there. Good luck!"

Following her instructions, I scan my pass and press the button for floor eleven. The lift shoots upward and a small thrill of anticipation bubbles within me. Within thirty seconds, the lift stops and the doors open into a dark office.

Cautiously, I step out, hoping not to trip or otherwise make a fool of myself before the day even begins.

I hesitate; there's no chatter, just a corridor of glass meeting rooms reflecting my own outline back at me.

I check my phone: 7:45 a.m.

I walk down towards the main office, my heels clicking far too loudly in the silence.

I leave my bag on an empty desk as I'm drawn by the scent of coffee coming from the kitchen. Taking a step forward, I freeze.

A quiet, hushed voice and footsteps pacing catch my attention. I press myself against the wall, my heart pounding in my chest. I don't want to be seen as a snoop on my first day.

"Yes… leave it to me. I'll have him out of here for inappropriate relations with an employee."

My stomach lurches.

Edging around the corner, my eyes catch the back of a shirtless man with his top draped around his neck. My eyes follow the line of his body down, resting upon his legs.

His calves. My brain short circuits to the encounter in the car park, those same muscular legs. Cyclist legs.

"Here, at the office. Got here early, made my first move in the car park talking to his new play thing."

I'm fairly certain that Luke is referring to me and Tyler, but what I don't understand is why. This is Tyler's business, so why or rather how would he plan to remove him?

An unwelcome thought creeps in, unless this isn't about business. Unless it's personal.

I reach for my phone and instinctively type Tyler's name. The thought of him calms me; he'll know what to do.

I press call. Nothing happens. No ringtone, it's just dead. I try again with no luck.

The man suddenly stops pacing and turns around. Like a rabbit caught in headlights, I step back, an exhale escaping me before I can swallow it.

I slink past my desk, into the toilets, finding safety for *now*.

CHAPTER 16 - A TASTE OF CONTROL

Forty-five minutes later, I emerge from the ladies' toilets, my hair now frizzed into an untamed halo of curls.

Note to self: no one arrives early at this office. Lesson learnt.

The office is alive now. Phones ring, keyboards clack. A few colleagues lift their eyes, smiling politely. On my desk, there's a brown envelope with my name scrawled on it.

Good morning Cass,
Welcome to Sparks Developments. Please bring yourself to my office so we can plan the week.
Tyler

Formal and curt, enough to make my pulse stutter. Tucking my bag under the desk, I straighten my jacket and walk towards the only office on the floor.

Knocking on the door lightly, my hands clam up as I await a response.

"Come in," a deep voice calls.

I step through the door and the woody bite of his aftershave hits me, warm and invasive, clinging to the air as if he owns it. Tyler sits behind his desk, broad shoulders at ease, but his attention locks onto me the moment I step inside. His green eyes scan over me, like he's already picking up on everything I'm trying to hide.

He raises a hand without taking his eyes off me, a quiet *one minute* gesture that somehow feels like an order. His other hand grips his phone, knuckles flexing as he speaks quietly into it.

"Yes," he says into the phone, voice low. "I don't care how early it is," he pauses. "Just get it sorted."

My fingers twist into each other and Tyler hangs up the phone without saying goodbye.

"Good morning, Cass."

I settle into the chair opposite him, the leather cool beneath my thighs. The office feels almost painfully clinical, with sterile walls and not a single personal touch anywhere. No photos, no clutter, nothing that hints at a life beyond these four walls.

"I'm glad you found your desk. One of the girls will show you around later. In the meantime, let's get you up to speed."

He pulls a chair from his side of the desk and places it next to him. "You'll need to see my screen."

He retrieves a laptop, sliding it across the desk. "When you're ready," he encourages, gesturing towards the chair.

I take a seat and cross one leg over the other, accidentally grazing his lower leg. His keyboard tapping pauses, just for a second, and I catch him clenching his jaw.

Opening the laptop and logging in, my eyes widen at the password scrawled on a post it: *Toot2025*.

"This isn't going to stick," I mutter.

Tyler peers over, teeth flashing in a playful grin. "Not a clue what you're talking about, Cass."

For the next hour and a half, we plough through notes, calendars, deadlines and people of interest. Tyler studies me in quiet intervals, eyes distant, almost young.

Tyler has been thorough, and whilst I appreciate the attention to detail, my fingers certainly do not.

I close the laptop abruptly. "Thanks for your help, Tyler. Maybe I can check in later?"

He taps on his phone, not looking up. "I'll let you know. Good luck on your first day."

He's back behind the mask he wears, nothing like the Tyler who looked at me like he was finally letting himself be seen.

I retreat to my desk, trying to think clearly, whilst my inner self rolls her eyes for being overly attentive to all the details.

Under my mouse, there's another note.

Picking it up, the front is signed '*Cass*', the writing is cursive and untamed.

'Welcome! Hope you haven't been overwhelmed. I can only handle ten-minute intervals with that one… ha ha.
I'm Maddie, desk to your right. IM me if you need anything, maybe lunch later.
Mads x'

Looking to my right, a petite blonde with a sleek bob meets my gaze and waves and comfort floods through me like a warm blanket.

Maybe, just maybe, this work placement won't be a complete disaster and I'll even become a note-leaver myself.

Hope is a dangerous thing to have.

CHAPTER 17 - CROSSING THE THRESHOLD

Blowing a stray strand of hair from my face, I push the last highlighted lease off my desk and let out a quiet cheer. Blue ink stains my fingers, proof of my triumph, and for the first time this week, I feel a flicker of Friday excitement.

I wander toward the toilets, needing a moment to myself, to freshen up. There's been little time to think about anything else this week, especially Tyler.

Having access to his diary has been torture. Like placing a decadent cake in front of someone on a diet and, of course, I caved and checked it daily, sometimes multiple times. All it displayed was a continuous busy status marked as *"Busy w/ Teddy."*

I tried to decipher it. Code name for a holiday? His actual Teddy? A woman? Avoiding me?

My scribbled list, hastily jotted whilst on hold earlier, was immediately scrunched up and discarded.

I'm applying a spritz of perfume to my wrists when Maddie breezes into the toilets.

"There you are! Thought you might have sneaked off on me."

Maddie, always energetic, is a breath of fresh air. On Wednesday, I agreed to meet her for drinks after work today, although part of me had secretly hoped she'd forgotten.

A quiet bath, a glass of wine... bliss.

"The bar on the top floor is cosy," she says, leaning into the mirror. "A nice way to meet people. That's how I met most of the office."

She shrugs, applying lipstick, hair bouncing with her movements. "It's intense here sometimes, as you've seen, but you smashed it this week. You've got a knack for this."

A blush creeps up my cheeks. A week of dealing with clients I could've happily launched out a window hasn't exactly been glamorous, but apparently, I've earned points.

"Thanks Maddie. As long as the bar is fully stocked, then I'm looking forward to it," I joke.

She laughs and gestures for me to follow her, leading the way through the office to the lifts.

We get in the lift and Maddie swipes her card, before pressing a button and the lift begins to climb.

We step onto the roof terrace and I'm pleasantly surprised. It's fully covered, heated and lined with high glass windows that frame the city lights in the distance.

Settling at a table for four, Maddie surveys the crowd. "Most faces you don't recognise are from other floors. People usually don't stay long here," she leans in, all conspiratorial. "First round's on me. Want to share a bottle of bubbles?"

"Absolutely," I grin, already picturing prosecco touching my lips.

Maddie's twenty, fresh out of sixth form, but she's sharp and ambitious. She's studying for her IRPM property exam and smart enough to have the company fund it. Long-term, she wants to become a surveyor and I can't help but respect her for that.

Our glasses clink.

"To surviving my first week," I declare.

"And to making new friends," Maddie adds.

Usually, I avoid drinking at work events, having seen colleagues unravel spectacularly at previous workplaces. Tonight, I deserve this.

By 7:30 p.m., most of the crowd has dispersed. Maddie slips off to the bathroom and I pull out my phone to text Lola, who's on holiday with James. Before I get a chance to put my phone away, it buzzes.

'Hey hun, Italy's amazing! Won't be back tomorrow—James has more meetings in France so going there for a few days. Can't wait to show you what I've bought!'

A pang of jealousy sinks in. I'm happy for her, but it's hard not to feel left behind. My gut still whispers caution about James.

Maddie returns from the bar, accompanied.

"Cass this is Luke. He works in contracts and new business."

Luke. I haven't seen him since Monday, or forgotten entirely what I overheard early that morning. His eyes are glacial and the way he arranges his face is too precise and careful.

"Actually, we've already met," I say, taking his hand. His handshake is rough and jolting and I jerk my hand back quickly.

Attempting to laugh off my nerves, we settle at the table. Luke sits a little too close and Maddie chats away beside us. I realise he hasn't shared much about himself at all. Shifty... or just shy.

"I think I'm going to go easy and get a Coke. Anyone want a drink?" I ask, standing.

Maddie cups her hands around her mouth. "I'm just trying to figure out what grumpy pants is doing here," she whispers, tipping her chin towards the corner of the room she's watching.

I laugh, following her gaze.

Tyler.

His presence has a sobering effect.

Luke watches my reaction from the corner of his eyes.

I wave down a waiter for a glass of water instead.

"Mads, most bosses have a stick up their arse," I deflect.

"Hmm... I just think he's unusually unusual," Maddie giggles.

Luke glances at Tyler like he's sizing him up. "I think I have to agree with Cass on this one. Sometimes you just don't like someone because there's not much to like."

My brow furrows, what a weird comment to make. Not subtle or disguised as banter... like he's thrown it out there on purpose, just to see how we'll react.

Tyler walks over and stands tall next to our table.

"Evening, Maddie, Luke, Cass. I just wanted to congratulate Cass on a successful first week," his eyes scan the three empty bottles of prosecco on the table. "Mind if I join you for one."

It's a statement, not a question and he slides in next to Maddie.

Luke suddenly stands and tips a flute of prosecco onto my lap.

"Shit!" I mop up the mess, waving him off.

"Sorry Cass."

Luke holds out a napkin out to me and I bat his hand away. "Not a problem," I force a smile.

"I've got to head out, thanks for a great evening, Maddie, Cass," a brief pause follows, "Tyler."

Turning on his heels, Luke escapes out of view to the lifts.

Maddie is hanging on for dear life, facing away from Tyler and I lean over to make sure she's okay, Maddie grabs my wrist.

"Mmm okay just want to rest my eyes."

Sitting back down in my seat, I lift my empty glass to Tyler. "To you, who can clear a room almost as soon as you arrive."

His mouth quirks, and the space he fills soothes the restlessness in me that has been flaring all evening. I've missed his presence more than I care to admit.

"I just wanted to congratulate you," he continues, voice lower now, meant for me alone. "For holding the fort. Signing a new client on day three out of five," his eyes hold mine. "Not easy."

"Too busy with Teddy this week to congratulate me in person, huh?" I tease.

Tyler doesn't answer, but his shoulders edge down slightly and his mouth flattens as if he's smoothing down a reaction.

"I think Maddie needs a cab. Let's call one." Tyler's phone clicks away, and we guide the petite, yet surprisingly heavy Maddie toward the lifts.

The Uber waits in the car park and with Maddie safely inside, I exhale.

"How about I get you home?" Tyler asks, the scent of lime and woody aftershave hitting me full force.

"Mhmm," I murmur, tipsy and flirtatious. "If the boss says so..." I salute. Tyler smiles, guiding me to his motorbike.

My adrenaline spikes. The last time on this bike was...hard to forget.

"No funny business," I warn, stepping into him by accident.

He chuckles, handing me a helmet. "Come on. Hold me tight. I underestimated how drunk you'd be."

As I slide my arms around his waist, an instinctive whisper inside urges me to run, but... I hold on tighter.

Hiccupping, I settle against his back, helmet on, as the roar of the engine carries us into the night.

Halfway through the ride, his voice drifts back to me, barely audible through the wind. "You did good this week... better than you know. When things get chaotic," he admits, almost more to himself than me. "It's... nice to have someone steady around."

There's a strain in his words, like he's bruised beneath them.

"Been a long time since I've had that." He cuts himself off, shoulders tensing, the moment closing as quickly as it came, like he regrets letting the truth slip through.

However, I heard it, and it tugs at something deep in my chest, even as a warning stirs at the back of my mind.

Careful, Cass. Men like Tyler don't show cracks unless there's a storm following closely behind.

CHAPTER 18 - CAUGHT IN THE MIDDLE

I stumble through the front door as Tyler flicks on the living room light behind me. The rush of air from the bike ride home has sobered me somewhat, and I pour myself a glass of water, letting it wash over my taste buds in a welcome rush.

"In my flat twice in one week... this is becoming a habit..." I tease. "Would you like a drink?" I ask, turning to face him.

His smile reaches his eyes. "I'd kill for a good cup of tea."

I put the kettle on and retrieve two mugs from the cupboard.

"Feel free to make yourself comfortable," I gesture toward the sofa as I fuss over our drinks, squeezing the tea bags and tossing them into the bin before bringing the steaming mugs to the coffee table.

Sitting down next to him, the sofa dips under our combined weight, nudging us slightly closer. Tyler scratches the back of his head and leans forward to pick up his mug.

"Thank you," his eyebrows lift slightly as he takes a sip.

The awkward formalities are thick enough to taste and I find myself fiddling with the rings on my index finger.

"I just wanted to say I'm sorry for giving you the wrong impression, Cass," Tyler confesses, his eyes finally locking with mine.

"I know this whole move hasn't been ideal, and I don't want you to think this is a game." He places his mug on the table, leaning forward with his elbows on his knees. "You're better than all of this… and I just really think I made a mistake."

A bitter taste rises in my mouth.

Mistake.

"Look, Tyler… I'm not really sure what I was expecting from this…" I bite back, repositioning myself on the sofa, holding onto the backboard for support.

"I agree. I think this has been a mistake. You're my boss now and I don't mix personal and work life, so I'm glad we can agree on something," my words slice through the air.

Tyler turns to face me, a crease forming between his brows. The green of his eyes darkens, and I find myself trapped in his gaze, unable to look away.

He stifles a laugh. "I was referring to my AWOL approach during your first week, not… our situation, but thank you for making that abundantly clear."

Our situation.

I watch him run his hands through his hair, noticing their size, hands I've felt brush past mine in ways I can't forget.

"Look, Tyler, you have your own life. Totally separate from mine. It's not my business who you're seeing. Teddy, or whoever she is, must be pretty special."

Tyler stiffens. "Snooping isn't a quality I admire Cass."

He pushes off the sofa, moving towards the balcony and pauses, staring out over the dark courtyard.

"Christ Cass, you're so confusing."

He turns, coming back to the sofa, lines of disappointment crease his face.

My stomach drops, spiralling the way it does at the top of a rollercoaster seconds before the plunge.

"You act interested... then you don't. You let me kiss you then..." He sighs. "I just don't get you."

I open my mouth, but nothing comes out.

"I don't even understand why I feel like this about someone who gives nothing back, but here we are."

I drop my eyes to the floor as they fill with hot tears.

Tyler picks up his jacket from the sofa.

"You know, I don't owe you an explanation, but contrary to everyone's belief, I like to think I'm a decent human being. Teddy is my nephew and my prick of a sister is a junkie."

He hesitates, fingers tightening on the collar of his jacket.

"Some mistakes don't just disappear because you want them to. I've been trying to put things right, clean up messes I should've handled years ago."

Zipping his jacket, he strides toward the front door, slamming his palm against it as he rests his head against the wood. "Every time I get close to what I want, something else blows up in my face."

My mind flashes back to when a different hand slammed against a different door with a violence meant to rattle me to pieces.

It wasn't him. Not the man standing at my door now, but my body didn't know the difference.

The knock had come out of nowhere back then, a hard, jolting crack that made the picture frames tremble on the wall.

"Cass," my ex had called through the door, voice deceptively soft. "Come on. Open up."

His palm had struck the wood again, loud and punishing, as though the door itself had offended him.

I remembered backing away, my pulse thundering in my ears. "Go home," I whispered, even though I knew he couldn't hear me, even though I knew he wouldn't.

The doorknob had turned slowly, deliberately. He was testing. Checking to see how far he could push.

"Don't be difficult," he said, sighing like I was inconveniencing him.

"You know I don't like it when you hide."

The worst part of it all wasn't the anger, it was the calm.
The patience in his voice that always came just before he broke something: a glass, a chair... me.

Eventually, he left, but the echo of that threat stayed with me.

Tyler's voice snaps me back to the present.

"This is what drugs do. They take someone good and hollow them out, and the world just lets it happen," he mutters.

Swallowing, my throat is dry and I can't find my voice.

The man that stands in front of me is not the same person, but my body doesn't know that.

"Strictly professional from now on Cass. The line is clear."

The door slams shut. I stare at it, then press my hands against my eyes as the tears sting my skin.

"Arghhh!"

I grab the tea towel and hurl it at the door, the action accomplishing nothing. Anger bubbles inside me. What is wrong with me, why can't I just let someone open up?

I steady myself on the kitchen counter as I breathe in and out. I can't leave it like this. Tyler's compassion, even as a boss, has been more welcome than anything else I've ever known.

I push my hair back, snatch my keys off the side and rush to the lift. The alcohol is still tingling through my veins and I force myself to swallow down the nausea clawing up my throat.

The lift numbers crawl upward.

"Fuck this."

I bolt for the stairwell, down two steps at a time, through the main lobby and out into the courtyard. Tyler's bike is still there.

I pace toward the opposite block, stopping in the shadows, squinting at my flat across the courtyard. The balcony... second floor... yes, I'm sure that's where I saw him.

Doubt creeps in, but frustration wins as I pick up bark from a nearby planter and hurl it at the balcony. It scatters like confetti.

Closing my eyes, I jump, slam my foot down, grab another handful and fling it into the air. This is madness. Romeo and Juliet level madness.

"Cass?"

The voice stops me cold. Pushing myself out of the planter, I turn to find Tyler standing at the entrance of his building, smirk hidden behind his hand. Dirt smudges my cheeks and clothes.

"Cass, you're covered in dirt."

"I... I was looking for something," I stammer, self-conscious, hands smoothing my wild hair.

He stands with his hands in his pockets. "Do you want to come in and clean up?"

"Yes," I blurt. "Please."

Tyler holds open the door to the front of his building, and a mixture of excitement and fear washes over me equally.

I'm going into Tyler's flat.

As he turns to continue forward towards the lift, I risk a look back at the planter that I was half buried in and flip my middle finger up at it.

Not today planter. Not today.

CHAPTER 19 - BOUND BY THE FIRE

Tyler switches on a lamp as we walk through his front door, the hue illuminating the room, casting shadows in the far corners behind the sofa.

Surprisingly, Tyler's flat feels much more homely than I had imagined.

To the right of the room, there is an L-shaped deep green sofa, complemented by plush gold and cream cushions. On the coffee table, there is a gold mirrored plate holding a lone candle and a TV remote. His walls are bare of pictures, apart from a lone rectangular mirror positioned behind the sofa.

An aroma of lemon lingers in the air. Stifling a chuckle, I was expecting a much more manly scent.

I glance over at Tyler, who is watching me intently.

"Feel free to make yourself comfortable," he gestures towards the sofa. "The bathroom is just on the right, same as your place, if you still want to get cleaned up."

"Thanks," I smile and kick off my boots, placing them next to the front door.

Locking myself in the bathroom, I catch sight of my face in the cabinet mirror and barely contain a yelp.

My mascara has smudged, leaving me with panda eyes and a line of dried dirt on my left cheek makes me look like I'm ready for paintball.

Running the tap, I stare at my reflection in disbelief. I look awful, no wonder Tyler invited me in to get cleaned up.

I need better mascara.

Opening the mirrored cabinet, I nose through the contents and find a men's face wash. I squeeze a blob into my hands and lather it between my palms so I can rinse my face. The smell of lime engulfs me as I recall the scent on Tyler, mixed with his aftershave.

Patting my face dry with a towel, I ready myself to face him.

Tyler is sat on the sofa with his leg bent, ankle leaning on his knee watching TV.

"I took the liberty of pouring a *very* weak drink for you... to take the edge off."

"Thank you."

"Look I just wanted to apologise for how I reacted back there. I didn't mean it. I... you just have this way of throwing me off balance."

A nervous laugh escapes me. "Tyler, look, I'm not very good with talking, so let me just get this out as I think it's time to explain a few things."

Picking up my glass of liquid luck, I drink it in one and place it back on the coaster.

Tyler's eyes flicker from me to my empty glass and back, fingers tapping his leg rhythmically.

"I'm not the biggest people person. I live far enough from my family so that no one drops by and the only person I can handle in moderate doses has been Lola."

I pause and fiddle with my middle ring finger. I could really do with another drink right now.

"I throw myself headfirst into work and let the world go by quite happily, knowing that I've made a difference in my own bubble."

Examining Tyler's face for permission to continue, he dips his head ever so slightly, encouraging me.

Instinctively, I reach for my glass and hesitate, remembering it's empty.

Tyler lifts his drink and offers it to me. I take it from his hand, our fingertips brushing for a split second. A flutter of nerves sparks low in my stomach, his touch is warm in comparison to the ice-cold glass, raising goosebumps along my skin.

"Thank you," I breathe.

"A client invited a few of us once to his place in the Lake District."

Taking a sip of my drink, the fuzzy effects of the alcohol start to take the edge off, filling me with false confidence.

Breathing in deeply, I close my eyes in an attempt to fend off the tears that fill them.

"Someone I had previously dated for a while was on this trip too. It was awkward; he was a prick so things didn't end well as he started being pretty controlling and handsy."

Opening my eyes, Tyler's body is rigid, one hand fisted over the other.

"After one of the group nights out, when I went to the bar where we were out of the eye of people, he tried to kiss me and I pushed him off, apologised for maybe having led him on by just being nice."

My stomach coils and recoils inside me and I don't know whether I need more drink or to throw up. Maybe both.

Shuffling forward on the sofa, closing the gap between Tyler and me, I place my hand on top of his and unclasp it. Holding his hand, palm towards me, I entwine my fingers with his and tilt my head forward, dropping my hair over my right shoulder.

Breathing in, steadying myself, I close my eyes and slowly guide our hands to the base of my neck, allowing his fingers to trace the four-inch scar that serves as my daily reminder of what he did to me.

After a few seconds, Tyler pulls his hand away slowly.

Catching his gaze, he no longer looks angry but sad, like he's sorry for me. Exactly what I didn't want.

Silently, tears spill from my eyes. Tyler's hand cups my chin, his thumb sweeping them away before he pulls me into his chest. I fold into him, my breath heavy and broken, sobbing softly against his shirt as he holds me there.

Before I get a chance to move away, Tyler squeezes me in his embrace and plants a kiss on the top of my head.

Tilting my head back, bringing our faces inches apart, I pause for a moment to take him in. The reflection from the light of the TV dances across his eyes. The lines around his eyes are too deep for someone his age, making me wonder what hardships he has encountered and a creeping 5 o'clock shadow darkens his jaw. Lifting my hand, I trace my finger along his jaw and watch as he clenches and unclenches at my touch.

"I don't want your pity, Tyler. I want you to understand why I pulled away from you that night," I sigh. "I'm not, not interested... I just don't find trusting people easy."

His hand cups around my chin, guiding me to him, and when he kisses me it's slow and unhurried. His lips stay on mine for a few seconds longer before he pulls away.

"Have you ever heard from him?"

I shake my head, wiping my nose with the end of my sleeve.

Our eyes meet and Tyler lets out a sigh. "Come here toot."

In a swift, deliberate motion, Tyler pulls my leg over him.

Positioned on his lap, he pulls me in close enough that the quick rise of his breath caresses my chest and his hands anchor me in place. Firm, like he's been waiting for this moment as long as I have.

My heartbeat stumbles as he brushes my hair back, his fingers grazing the side of my face before settling at the base of my neck, guiding me towards him with gentle pressure. His eyes meet mine in the low light. They're dark and burning with a want so clear it steals the air from my lungs.

Our kiss is unrestrained, as if he's been holding back and finally letting his emotions pour out. His hand trails along my side, slow but purposeful, the warmth of his touch igniting every nerve it touches.

I move with him without thinking, drawn into the heat of his body and the gravity of him. Every shift pulls us closer, until it feels like neither of us can pull away even if we tried. My hips sway instinctively, keeping pace with our kiss and I need more.

My hands slide to the hem of his T-shirt, fingers curling into the fabric. I tug, and he breaks the kiss just long enough to let me. His arms instinctively lift, and I pull it up and over his head, hurried and clumsy with desire.

My palms meet his bare skin and everything in me stills. Ink stretches across the left side of his chest, half-hidden in the low light. I can't make it out properly, but my fingers hesitate over it, tracing the outline.

Tyler's eyes meet mine with a hunger flickering behind them, like he's trying to decide if he's already past the point of stopping.

One of his hands slides to my lower back, the other bracing my hip. He moves us smoothly, guiding me down, turning me with a single, steady motion until my back meets the cushions and he's above me, close enough that I can feel the heat of him everywhere.

His eyes search my face, his mouth hovering over mine like he's seeking permission. When he kisses me again, it's slower, deeper, as if he wants me to feel how badly he's been holding back.

Breaking for air, our lips hover a breath apart, ragged and uneven and our foreheads rest against one another as if neither of us are quite ready to let go.

Unhooking myself from his embrace, I settle my head against his chest, letting the warm steady thump of his heartbeat calm my own.

"Cass, you're not the only one with secrets that hurt to talk about," he confesses, circling my shoulder with his fingers as I close my eyes.

I'd just lied to him.

I've heard from him on every birthday for the last seven years. I change my number and there's nothing for a while, long enough for me to think I might finally be free of him. Then he resurfaces, following up with a 'Happy Birthday' text or card in the post. There's always a second message, casual, with details from a holiday I've just returned from or the make of the car I'm now driving now. Quiet reminders that no matter how far I go, or how carefully I disappear, he's still watching.

Maybe I'm overthinking it, my birthday is coming up and that little niggle has crept back into my subconscious.

The thought of him leaves me feeling hollow.

"You continue to amaze me Cass."

Cuddling into Tyler's chest, I continue to listen as he talks, trying to relax against the rise and fall of his breathing.

Drifting off to sleep, an ache at the back of my mind reminds me that I cowered away. I did nothing about what happened. I told no one.

I let a monster roam free.

When Tyler's breathing settles into a slow, steady rhythm beneath my cheek, the ache in my chest doesn't ease, if anything, it sharpens.

Now that the heat of the moment has passed, the truth seeps in like cold water. I showed him the scar. I let him touch the part of me I hide from everyone, even myself some days, yet he held me like it mattered.

I can still feel the shadow of a different hand at the back of my neck, rough and punishing. I can still hear the smashing of plates in the kitchen, the slam of the door.

I swallow hard, fighting another wave of tears. What am I doing letting someone this close? Letting myself want someone who, no matter how soft he was tonight, still has shadows he won't name, living in a world I've only seen glimpses of and already don't trust.

I hate that I lied, that I'm still protecting the man who hurt me more than anyone should ever be hurt. I hate that even now, with Tyler's warmth wrapped around me, the fear of my ex finds me again.

His hand drifts across my shoulder in his sleep and I flinch, just a little, then let out a slow breath until the tension leaves my muscles.

Maybe he didn't notice.

Maybe tomorrow I can convince myself I imagined all of this.

Maybe tomorrow I can forget the way he looked at me, like I wasn't ruined.

Until tiredness consumes me, I lie awake in his arms, caught between the past I ran from and the future I'm too scared to reach for.

CHAPTER 20 - TANGLED IN HIM

I stretch my arms above my head, and before I can fully remember where I am, I roll straight off the sofa and onto the floor, cocooned in a blanket like a burrito.

"Ow-shit."

A low laugh warms the air above me.

My eyes snap open, staring at the ceiling, and an upside-down Tyler steps into my line of sight, causing me to inwardly groan. A shirtless, tanned Tyler with damp hair pushed back and a towel slung low around his waist.

His mouth twitches. "Going to stay down there all day or do you want some toast?"

I manage a noise, attempting to salvage the little pride that remains.

Sitting up, I pull myself onto the sofa using my elbows, keeping the blanket wrapped around my legs. Tyler leans forward, placing the plate on the coffee table, before dropping onto the sofa beside me.

I am painfully aware of the small space between us and the fact that he has not yet put on a shirt, or trousers for that matter.

I devour my toast and my stomach growls betrayingly loud.

Tyler tilts his head. "I didn't realise you're such a fidgety sleeper," he confesses, resting his arms behind his head. His biceps flex but I pretend not to notice.

"How do you know I fidget?"

"You elbowed me twice," he replies casually. "Kicked me once and at one point you stole the entire blanket. Impressive for someone your size."

My cheeks burn. "You can't hold me responsible for actions committed in my sleep."

He smirks, eyes drifting over my face in a strangely gentle way. "As long as you don't make a habit of stealing my sleep either."

As I push myself off the sofa, I replay the events of last night in my head, heart hammering like it's run a marathon.

Tyler taps away on his mobile, distracted, but his presence fills the whole flat.

The kettle clicks, and the silence becomes almost deafening.

"I should head out," I mumble. "Let you get on with your day."

Tyler approaches the breakfast bar, water droplets trickling from his damp hair onto his chest as he moves, phone in hand, completely absorbed in whatever he's doing.

I can't tear my gaze away, tracing every curve and contour, as a soft pull tugs at my insides. My mind drifts back to our first business meeting, him sitting across from me with his top button undone.

I step closer to Tyler, still distracted by his mobile, to get a better look.

On his left peck there's a tattoo etched into his skin, every detail meticulously captured. The tree stands tall, its branches laden with leaves, while it looks as though a storm is brewing in the background. The black and white hues enhance the realism, with leaves appearing to be swept away by the fierce winds, creating a scene that seemed almost alive.

I pause, pondering what it might mean to him. There's a weight in the image, a resilience that feels familiar, as if the tree is standing against something unseen, much like Tyler himself.

I'm unaware of Tyler's watchful eyes upon me.

"See something you like?" Tyler leans with one hand on the counter.

"That's an impressive tattoo…" I admit, nodding towards the left side of his chest.

He hesitates for a brief moment, almost unnoticeable, before pulling his T-shirt from the back of the breakfast bar stool and sliding it over his head.

"Yeah… It's just a tattoo."

His words are clipped and almost defensive, but his eyes flick briefly to his chest as if it conceals something unspoken, a memory or promise he's not yet willing to share.

"Tyler, thanks for last night… See you Monday?"

Closing the space between us, Tyler pulls me into his chest, his chin resting at the top of my head and I feel a deep sigh escape him.

"I know last night was a lot," he says quietly, "but if you're worried I regret any of it…" he shakes his head once, "I don't."

My throat goes dry.

"And if you're worried I expect anything from you this morning…" His voice dips. "I also don't."

The tension in my shoulders eases slightly.

He reaches out, brushing a stray strand of hair behind my ear.

"You don't have to run from me," he says, his voice soft.

"I'm not running," I whisper, but the hesitancy in my voice betrays me.

"Maybe not your feet," he murmurs, "but your mind's already sprinting out the door and down the hallway."

I look up at him as the morning light catches his green, unarmoured eyes and I smile, but do not reply.

"Monday," Tyler plants a light kiss at the top of my head.

Opening the door, I peer back into the flat and Tyler already has his mobile to his ear with his back turned.

Pulling the door shut behind me, I almost break into a light jog to get back to my flat.

Headphones in, the hot bath water burns my skin as I relax in the bath to my Spotify playlist.

The scent of Tyler's facewash lingers, and I feel guilty washing it away, as if I'm erasing the memory that last night actually happened.

Having been in the bath for over 30 minutes, my skin is beginning to shrivel as I feel the water cooling.

Twisting the tap with my toe to add a blast of hot water, *Ariana Grande – Dangerous Woman* beings playing in my ears. I pull my hand out of the bath, sorry Ari, not a bit of me.

Before I get the chance to press the skip button, the chorus kicks in full blast and I settle back into the hot water, pushing the bubbles around the bath with my hands.

Is this how it's going to be now? Even song lyrics reminding me of Tyler.

I imagine Lola's face if I confided in her about this. I can see it now: a fake gag, putting two fingers to her mouth, rolling her eyes.

I had kept my Saturday free because Lola was supposed to be coming over, but now that she's away for another week, I have the entire afternoon and evening to myself.

Relieved to have some time to myself, I seize the chance to indulge in some self-pampering.

An hour and a half later, I've managed to wash and dry my hair, do a face mask, put a load of laundry on, and I'm now in bed with the last series of Vampire Diaries on in the background while I paint my toenails.

Damon Salvatore's chiselled face fills my TV screen, and the resemblance to Tyler makes my mind wander.

It's only been six hours since I was at his flat and I'm struggling to ignore the unsettling feeling in my chest that I haven't heard from him.

When did I ever wait around to hear from someone? The answer was never, but now, I can't help but wonder what he's up to.

Unwilling to give in, I push my phone aside.

Sitting back in bed, I wiggle my toes in approval at their new colour, impressed by how good they look. My phone buzzes with a message, and excitement washes over me at the prospect that it might be Tyler.

Lola: *'Don't think I've forgotten about your birthday. I'll be back on Sunday!'*

Messages from Lola have become rare treasures lately and my heart softens with a quiet wave of relief knowing we'll finally get to spend time together next week.

Lola: 'Any juicy gossip you want to share with me about the scandalous relationship you're having with your new boss?!'

I tap out a quick reply.

'Lol relationship is a bit of an overstatement…stayed over his last night though…..'

Lola: *'You dirty stop out, I need the full story!!!'*

Carefully stepping into my living room, mindful not to smudge the polish drying on my toes, I place my phone on charge and drift towards the balcony.

Lola has been away for a while now, her trip keeps getting extended due to James's busy schedule. While I'm none the wiser about holiday details, I'm just glad she's been messaging me so I know she's okay.

Still, a creeping discomfort has made itself at home in me whenever I think of our exchange before she left.

I lean against the balcony door and glance out across the courtyard.

March has always felt like a promise to me. It's only 2:30 p.m with a generous hour and a half of daylight still clinging to the day, but the evenings start to stretch a little longer, the air carries hope and tiny bursts of colour begin to push through the soil. Even when the rain comes, and it usually does, it feels like we're inching closer to summer, to warmth, to something new.

The landline rings, cutting through the silence. There's only one person still stubbornly calling me on that relic.

My sister.

I hover over the ringing telephone for a second before answering.

"Hello,"

"Hey Cass, are you okay? I messaged you last night, but you didn't reply."

"I'm okay, sorry work has been a little bit manic… I got moved to a new…"

"Oh great, so mum and dad wanted me to ask if you're free tonight to go for your birthday dinner, so I thought I'd ask you, although I told them you'd probably be busy since you hate celebrating your birthday anyway."

A flare of heat rises in my chest.

"Actually, that sounds great. What time?"

"Oh… you're free?" she pauses. "Ehm, let's say 7pm I'll let Mum and Dad know. How about that Chinese place on Loughton High Street? Let me call them and book now."

"Err yeah sure… sounds great"

"Perfect, see you later."

I hear the beeping tone in my ear before I even manage to say goodbye, and I shake the phone aggressively, letting out a shriek of annoyance.

It's been nearly two weeks since my last cigarette, but the craving hits me so hard it almost knocks the air from my chest.

Desperately, I thrust my hands into the pockets of my coat hanging on the rack by the front door, overwhelmed by an aching urge to burn through an entire pack in one go.

Bingo. I fish out an open packet of cigarettes, throw on my coat and practically float out to my balcony.

I sink into the chair, rest my feet up on the railing and slide a cigarette between my lips. The first inhale scorches down my throat and painfully blooms in my lungs. I close my eyes and lean back, letting the smoke unfurl from me in a long, unsteady exhale, leaving me a little dizzy.

What a shit show tonight is going to be.

I haul myself inside to get ready, closing the balcony door and pulling the curtains shut.

I can handle Bea… It's Tyler I'm not sure I can survive.

CHAPTER 21 – THE THING'S I DON'T SAY

Tyler

I am not the same person I once was.

I keep telling myself this tonight in the hope that at some point it sticks, but it would be so easy to slip back into old habits.

Tonight feels peaceful; I can hear traffic moving along the roads below from my balcony. Lights in the flats opposite flicker on and off, as domestic lives carry on normally, and somewhere down below, a couple walk past, their laughter echoing through the courtyard.

Cass's flat lights are on.

She's inside, I know that much, but her curtains are drawn.

I lean against the balcony railing, phone loose in my hand, listening to James update me on a situation I already half understand.

"It's not urgent," he says for the second time. "But I don't like the pattern."

"Neither do I," I reply quietly.

The pattern bothers me. Repeated occurrences always do. Small things most people would brush off: a name that keeps circling back to places it shouldn't, the same car with the same number plate lingering too often.

Too much of a coincidence.

Cass has been unsettled all week.

She hasn't said much outright, she wouldn't, but I notice the subtle changes: the way her attention splinters when her phone buzzes, the way she locks her door with deliberate care.

Someone learns that behaviour for a reason.

"Don't do anything yet," I tell James. "Just be available."

"Always am."

I end the call and slip the phone into my pocket.

It's cooler than usual tonight, with a damp chill clinging to the air, settling into everything it touches. The couple who passed by earlier are now seated on one of the benches below, leaning into each other and laughing. The air carries her laugh up to my balcony, carefree and light, and for a moment I envy them.

There's a black car idling near the corner, engine running, lights off. It's been there before, long enough to be a coincidence if you're feeling generous.

I am not generous.

I memorise the plate without thinking.

Straightening up, I shrug off my jacket, push my sleeves up and take a hard sip of whiskey, letting the burn settle.

I lean against the balcony handrail and scan the courtyard again; the car still hasn't moved.

Sighing heavily, I close my eyes and reach a decision.

I shrug into my jacket quickly, close the balcony door behind me, and head for the lift.

As I walk out of the building, I replay the last conversation I had with Cass, not for what we spoke about, but for what sat underneath it.

What unsettles me isn't her distance, it's the way she almost speaks, the pause before each reply, as if she's weighing up what it might cost her to tell the truth. People only do that when being heard has cost them something.

The memory of last night clings to me dangerously, like she wants this just as much as I do but doesn't trust herself to reach for it without flinching. I can still feel the weight of her against me, the sound of her breath changing when I kissed her like I meant it.

She's guarded, not cold and only ever gives people what they ask for rather than dish up information freely.

It's taken me years to realise that there's a difference.

I don't know her story yet, well not fully, but after what she confessed last night: her ex, the violence, it's impossible to ignore the gaps. She still hears from him, she made that much clear by volunteering too much information.

I won't pry, but I will protect. Protection creates space, and she needs that space to breathe.

My phone vibrates again. James.

"She's leaving the flat. Should we keep eyes on her?"

"Yes," I say, exhaling. "Let me know if there's anything I need to know about."

My jaw tightens, but I let it go just as quickly. Anger clouds my judgement and I need it to be razor-sharp right now.

I won't approach the car directly, that would be foolish. Instead, I pull the collar of my jacket up high and walk past, unhurriedly, phone to my ear like any other man heading out late.

I observe the driver's silhouette, noting how he stiffens when I pass and how his attention sharpens.

Predators notice other predators; his reaction tells me enough.

I keep walking, and when I reach the end of the street, I pause and turn around, heading back towards my flat.

Keeping to the shadows, I see Cass jumping into a cab outside her building.

Staying out of sight as the cab pulls away, it takes a left at the end of the road. Moments later the black car that had been idling near the corner pulls away from the kerb and turns left after it.

I retrieve my phone from my pocket and tap out a quick text to James.

Me: 'Number plate RJ23 HPP. Don't do anything yet just keep it on file.'

Moments later my phone buzzes.

James: 'Got you boss.'

Before I enter my building, I cast my gaze over to Cass's flat, which is now dark, and I consider how easy it would be for me to jump on my bike and catch up to her to check she was okay.

To follow the car that left soon after to see if my suspicions are correct, but I don't because that would be for me, not for her.

She doesn't need a man appearing in the night to save her. She needs to realise, in her own time, that someone is paying attention without demanding anything in return.

There's a difference between safety and control, and I've been on the wrong side of that line before, which I don't intend to cross again.

~

Lying in bed, I can't get comfortable. Something that's been circling in my mind for the last few days keeps surfacing.

Cass doesn't fit neatly in my life. She is different.

The old me wouldn't have hesitated to jump on my bike, follow the car and beat the shit out of the driver, even if he was innocent, just because I could.

I won't do that. I won't interfere unless she asks. Unless... the line is crossed.

If her safety is threatened, my restraint ends and I know that with absolute certainty.

My phone lights up on the bedside table next to me and I reach for it.

James: 'Someone's been testing the building. Doors, camera. It's not random.'

I stare at the screen for a moment. This isn't something I can ignore until the morning.

I swing my legs out of bed and drag a hand down my face as I type a reply that I don't send. My jaw tightens as I lock my phone and I throw back the covers as if they've offended me.

It's late, and I know I'll seem like I'm overreacting, but I'd rather appear that way than wake up to something I can't undo.

I'm on my feet before I can talk myself out of it, tugging my clothes on in the dark with movements that feel too sharp. I'm going in for security, for standard procedure and that's the truth, kind of.

What's taken me longer to admit, that sits beneath all the restraint and the rules that I keep forcing myself to follow, is that I don't just want her to let me in.

I want her to stay.

CHAPTER 22 - THE MASK SLIPS

Walking through the main reception of Sparks, I draw in a steady breath, as if oxygen alone can prepare me for another week in a building that still feels like borrowed territory.

It's been a busy week of site visits and I'm looking forward to having my feet planted at my desk after three long days away.

"Good morning, Charlie," I chirp, smoothing the sleeve of my blazer.

Charlie looks up from her screen, bright-eyed and warm as ever.

"Good morning! Don't you look lovely today."

A blush spreads across my cheeks. I'm dressed a bit bolder than usual today: a sharp red suit, a sheer white blouse, and nude pumps. Absolutely nothing to do with my dangerously handsome boss, whose office sits directly opposite me... of course not.

My birthday dinner over the weekend unfolded with painful predictability; Mum and Dad radiated warmth while Bea radiated boredom. She couldn't have made it more obvious that she had somewhere else she'd rather be.

The lift doors open into the near silent corridor. I walk towards the open-plan office, mentally stacking my to-do list like fragile glass but, as I round the corner, I freeze.

Tyler's office light is on.

I check my phone. 7:31 a.m.

I place my bag on my desk, my pulse fluttering at my neck, and cross to his door.

Two knocks. Nothing.

I lean into the wood, listen and knock again.

Silence settles in the pit of my stomach.

My fingers curl around the door handle before my brain catches up. The door yields with a long, low creak, spilling light into the quiet, dimly lit office.

Tyler slouches in his chair, his suit crumpled, shirt half undone, his tie abandoned on the floor. A half-empty bottle of Jack Daniel's sits beside a glass and a scatter of paper on his desk, the stale scent of whiskey hangs heavy in the air.

This isn't just a rough morning; it's evidence of a night he didn't expect anyone to witness.

I clear my throat more loudly than intended and Tyler stirs, lifting his arms to rest behind his head, his features drawn.

Instinctively, I step back, heat crawling across my skin.

"You are," he mutters, voice gravelly, "the loudest morning person alive."

A shiver ripples through me. "I... didn't think you were here."

He stretches, fingers locking behind his head again and a low groan unfurls.

"And you still came in? God, you love a snoop."

He gives a lopsided grin. Careless, unaware that even undone, he radiates a magnetic sharpness.

A small nervous laugh escapes me. "Well, it's a good job it was me who found you."

My gaze sweeps the desk again, lingering on the disarray. "Is everything okay?"

Tyler grabs the bottle and tucks it into the bottom drawer, his jaw tight.

"Honestly, Cass?" He pauses briefly, as if he's collecting his thoughts. "Last night wasn't just me blowing off steam," he mutters, rubbing the bridge of his nose.

"James called after hours. Some security detailing issues," he says, sighing heavily. "I missed something big, and now it's crawling back out of the woodwork and landing in my lap." He closes a folder a little too forcefully.

"I've been trying to fix it quietly. Clean up the mess before it affects us," he lifts his eyes to mine, raw and exhausted. "So, I stayed here. All night. Trying to work things out."

He starts gathering papers into a tidy pile, but his movements are overly precise. Too controlled. A man tidying up because something inside him is falling apart.

"Can I get you a coffee?" I ask, more to break the tension than out of courtesy. "I was going to get one myself…"

"That would be great," he says, still not quite meeting my eyes.

I escape into the kitchen, heart hammering against my ribs.

While the coffee machine warms up, I find myself drifting toward the east-facing window. The sun is rising just above the horizon, a thin gold light cuts through the gloom, and the city below looks deceptively peaceful.

A flicker of movement catches my eye. A figure in the car park. Hooded. Alone.

From here I can see my car tucked behind the bushes, beyond it, a gated car park I've never noticed, and inside sits a single motorbike.
Tyler's.

The figure crouches. A gloved hand slips beneath the gate, holding something small and a sharp burst of light flashes. Then the figure withdraws, glancing around before slipping out of sight with chilling purpose.

The coffee machine beeps repeatedly, drawing my attention back to the room.

Tyler isn't in his office when I return; his desk is now spotless. Only his mobile remains on the surface, vibrating insistently with a call from Peter. It rings out and then starts again.

I glance towards the half-open door leading out into the office, but there is still no sign of Tyler. Before I can second guess myself, I reach out and swipe to answer.

"Tyler, why don't you answer your fucking phone? We need to tighten security around her... her ex isn't just some jealous idiot. He's connected to people we really don't want to be involved with."

My heart stalls, but he keeps going, unaware.

That's why the threats escalated; he's got backing, but we don't know exactly from where yet.

Panicking, I hang up the phone and put it back on the desk.

"Thanks for the coffee," Tyler says from behind me, his voice clearer now. "I could smell it from down the hall."

I hold my breath, afraid Tyler might notice the look on my face that'll give me away.

He stands in the doorway, towelling off damp hair. He's transformed now, wearing crisp trousers, polished shoes and a white shirt unbuttoned just enough to reveal his tanned skin.

He appears composed again. Calm. The man from ten minutes ago has been erased, at least if not entirely, then buried.

I force a smile. "No problem." I need to leave before I give anything away.

"If you need anything today, I'll be... just outside."

Taking a sip of coffee, his gaze lands on me.

"Mmm. The fact that you make coffee this good will make it that much harder to ever let you leave," he jokes.

I offer a small smile in return.

As I turn to go, his phone rings again. *Peter.*

"Oh, quick question," I say, pausing. "Do we need to register our cars to park here? To avoid fines?"

Tyler pauses mid-buttoning his shirt, studying me.

"No. Parking's free."

"It's just... I saw someone taking photos of your motorbike earlier. Thought it might be traffic wardens."

He freezes, for a second, before finishing buttoning up with newly tense movements. His face hardens, strain pulling at the edges.

"Thanks, Cass."

I slip out of his office, closing the door behind me. His voice rises on the other side, low at first, then sharp enough to vibrate the wood.

At my desk, I open my laptop and try to drown myself in my inbox, but Peter's words keep replaying in my mind, the memory of the phone ringing relentlessly with a truth I was never meant to hear.

All this time, I thought I understood the risk. I thought leaving my ex meant the worst was already behind me, but it feels like I'm only just beginning to skim the surface of something bigger than the both of us.

What rattles me the most is the realisation that I'm not as free as I've been pretending. My past isn't finished with me. I wanted distance. Control.

Instead, I'm being pulled into the dark, and Tyler is already caught in it with me.

Tidying away loose papers on my desk, I pop my highlighters back in their drawer, eyes burning from a day of heavy reading.

Tyler has been in his office for most of the day, muffled voices and heightened conversations have escaped from behind the door at various intervals.

"Afternoon, Cass."

My head snaps up.

James.

He's standing there like normal, suited up, just like I remember him, phone in his hand.

Not sunburnt, not relaxed, and not halfway across Europe like he's supposed to be.

"You're not on holiday," I challenge, the words leaving my mouth without any thought.

A flicker of surprise darts across his face, well masked, but there.

He smiles, but its thin. "Change of plans."

My pulse picks up. "With Lola?"

The pause is so brief, it's barely there.

"She's...dealing with something," he says. "I'm just here for a meeting with Tyler."

The pieces slot together easily and I hate how quickly my mind fills in the gaps. Lola's phone lighting up, James standing in front of me, solid proof that she didn't just bend the truth; she broke it.

Tyler steps out of his office, his eyes darting between us.

"James," he says. "You're early."

James nods. "Didn't want to keep you waiting."

I sink further into my seat, suddenly aware that I am intruding on something I wasn't meant to see.

As James follows Tyler into his office, he glances over his shoulder once, worry etched on his face.

It confirms everything I've been sitting at the edge of.

She isn't on holiday, she's hiding, but the question is from who?

CHAPTER 23 - THE COST OF KNOWING HIM

A faint buzzing noise makes me stir, waking me from my dream. Covering my head with the duvet, I had forgotten to close the blinds last night, and light is streaming in through the window, catching me off guard.

The front door buzzer sounds again, more insistent this time as I fumble for my phone.

I quickly spot a text from Lola.

'Don't forget I'm popping over tomorrow! Miss you! HAPPY BIRTHDAY!'

10:55 a.m.

Lola is still pretending she's on holiday. I haven't mentioned my encounter with James to her, and it seems James hasn't said anything either. I don't want to push now; I'd prefer to catch her off guard tomorrow when I see her face to face.

Suppressing a groan, I peel back the duvet and slide my feet into my slippers. By the time I reach the door, the courier hastily thrusts a dark blue velvet box into my hands, with a gold ribbon tied around it, glinting as if something expensive and secret is inside. I sign for it without really looking at the pad.

Just as I go to close the door, something bright catches my eye.

Flowers.

A full bouquet of birds of paradise, my favourite, resting neatly beside the door frame as if they've been waiting patiently for me.

Balancing everything against my hip, I close the door with the back of my foot and carry the gifts to the breakfast bar. The flat, usually a soft quiet in the morning, feels unusually still.

I fetch a vase, fill it, and arrange the flowers inside, watching the orange and blue petals flare outwards like flames. They're perfect.

There's no note, no tag, not even a stray receipt, and a low knot forms in my stomach.

I tug at the gold ribbon on the velvet box. Inside, on a bed of midnight-blue tissue, lies a single rose. Beneath it, a black YSL clutch bag and a crisp white note.

Happy Birthday, Toot.
Table at 7pm. I'll pick you up at 6:30.
Any issues, let me know. —Tyler.

A fragile spark of hope flares, then dies, as I'm brought crashing back down to reality when I remember the phone call I'd overheard yesterday.

Part of me wants to accept, to step forward and see where this leads, yet another part warns that once I do, there's no going back. Perhaps I'm overthinking it, but hearing what Peter had to say has allowed doubt to creep in loudly.

My phone rings in the bedroom, and as if summoned, Tyler's name flashes on the screen. My thumb hovers momentarily before I decide to answer the call.

"Happy birthday Toot, hope you're enjoying your day off!" he booms before I can speak. "Courier just confirmed delivery."

For a heartbeat, I panic. Did the courier take one of those awful photos? Did he capture my chipped, gremlin toes?

I glance down. Fresh polish. Thank God.

"Thank you, Tyler," I manage, "It's…more than I expected. I don't even remember telling you when my birthday is."

"I mean, being the boss has perks," he jokes lightly, muffled voices echoing in the background.

My eyes drift towards the flowers suspiciously sitting on the side.

"So," I ask, "How did you know birds of paradise are my favourite?"

Silence follows my question for a moment too long.

"Flowers?" His tone shifts just enough to confirm my previous thoughts.

I force a bright, brittle tone. "My mistake. I'll be ready at 6:30. Looking forward to it!" I blurt out and hang up before he can say anything else.

Pressure builds behind my eyes. I cross to the bin, fishing out the flower wrapping like a madwoman. There has to be something I missed. A slip. A card. A name. *Anything.*

They're probably from Mum and Dad, I tell myself, but the lie tastes sour.

I pace the flat, phone in hand, opening and closing my messages as if I might find a clue there. I search for the florist faintly printed on the wrapping paper and call their number, but they're no help. No one left a name when they ordered them.

I begin tidying up, just to stay upright, wiping counters that are already clean, washing my mug that's already been washed. The minutes drag on, and going for a jog is the only thing that'll clear my mind.

Several hours later, after much deliberation and attempted distraction, my hair is in a crooked bun and every scrap of my bin's contents is strewn across the kitchen tiles. I'm kneeling like a deranged archaeologist, searching for a clue that refuses to exist.

My shirt presses against my back, and a fine sheen of sweat breaks across my temples.

I *need* to know who sent those flowers.

I've tried to convince myself I told Tyler once, in passing. Maybe after too many drinks, but the harder I dig through my memory, the more it resists.

There's only one other person who knows.

My hand instinctively reaches for the scar at the back of my neck, fingertips grazing over the raised skin.

I swallow, my throat tightening like a knot that has been pulled too quickly.

A knock at the door startles me.

6:30 p.m. on the dot.

Tyler and his maddening punctuality.

I yank my hair down from its bun and hurry to unlatch the door.

"Sorry, just give me a second."

I dive to the floor, sweeping the bin's contents back into the bag in a frantic blur, praying he didn't see.

"I, uh... didn't take you for the dumpster diving type," Tyler leans casually against the door frame, raising an eyebrow.

Tripping over my own feet in my haste to get off the floor, I slam the lid on the bin, snatch the clutch from the counter and breeze into the bathroom.

"Long story. I lost something. Let me just freshen up and I'll be right out," I shout over my shoulder.

Fighting with my makeup, trying not to take too long, my phone vibrates.

Luke? That's unexpected. I glance at the screen, hesitate briefly, and then answer.

"Cass," he says, sharp and clipped.

"Luke," I manage, forcing calm into my voice.

"I need that report from last week," he says. "I've asked twice and I still haven't received it."

"I'll get it to you first thing tomorrow, I'm not at work today," I say, trying to keep my voice steady.

"I need it before lunch tomorrow or it's going to be a problem for us both." His tone is flat and unwelcoming.

"Yes, of course. I can do that."

"Good," he says. "Don't let work slip, Cass. You know what happens when people get distracted."

The line goes dead before I can respond, irritation creasing my brows.

I finish my make up and cruise past Tyler on my way out of the bathroom, my new clutch under my arm. He follows, his eyes landing momentarily on the flowers sat on my kitchen side before closing the door behind us, and it confirms to me what I already knew.

The flowers are not from him.

Still in the dark about where Tyler is taking me tonight, I've started to wish I'd dressed up a little more. My sexy little jeans don't feel quite so sexy anymore and everything feels a little too tight and uncomfortable.

~

Stepping out of the car, I breathe in the welcomed fresh air after the twenty minute drive. Tyler's hand glides to the small of my back, a warm, confident touch that sends goosebumps skittering across my skin and lights a slow, smouldering ache low in my stomach.

"Glad you liked your present." Tyler flashes his gaze to the YSL bag hooked over my shoulder.

Ushering me towards an unmarked doorway, Tyler gently pushes it open with quiet confidence and signals for me to step inside. The space beyond is dim, the air thick with the low, sultry hum of jazz seeping through the walls. Shadows flicker across the floor as my eyes adjust.

Tyler moves ahead of me, weaving through the narrow entrance towards a dark green velvet curtain draped like a secret. He pauses, looks back at me, then slips a hand behind the fabric. His knuckles tap out a slow, deliberate rhythm, almost like a password.

A moment later, the curtain shifts and a hidden door nudges open, unleashing a surge of richer, deeper jazz that swells into the corridor. Tyler gives me a crooked, knowing grin before pushing aside the heavy velvet curtain and slipping inside. I swallow my nerves and follow.

The room beyond comes alive. Warm amber lights cast a glow over small round tables, and the air is filled with conversation and laughter. At the centre, a circular stage dominates the space, where a woman in a satin gown croons into a microphone, while the band leans into the music just behind her.

Tyler guides me through the maze of tables, stopping at one perfectly positioned in the centre of the room, offering a clear view of the stage. He pulls out a chair for me with an ease that feels both practised and unexpectedly intimate.

I slide into the seat, smoothing my hands over my thighs as he settles beside me, the gentle hum of the music wrapping itself around us like a promise.

"You know, the bag was a highly inappropriate gift to receive from my boss."

Tyler leans in close, his eyes lock onto mine with an intensity that captures my focus. With a gentle touch, he tucks a strand of hair behind my ear, his warm breath tantalisingly close.

"You know, it's also highly inappropriate to accept a gift from your boss and then go out on a date with him," he whispers, his voice tingling with allure.

Pulling back slightly to meet his gaze, I can't help but pout with a hint of annoyance.

"Touche," I roll my eyes playfully.

"You know, I was told this was just dinner," I say, letting the words hover between us. "It appears I was misled, and if this is a date...well, that's even more inappropriate."

Tyler's gaze lingers on me, intense and unwavering. His eyes flick down, tracing the curve of my lips for a fraction of a second, and I catch my own breath at the unspoken promise in that glance.

The boundary between professional decorum and personal intrigue was quickly dissolving into a haze of uncertainty.

I like him, and more than anything, I trust him and this situation is toying with my entire belief system.

The tension breaks when the waitress comes over to take our drinks order.

An hour and a half later, after three strong martinis, conversation with Tyler has been flowing effortlessly.

I refrain from interrupting him; each passing minute seems to lift a burden off his shoulders, allowing him to breathe more freely.

Tyler's family relations were minimal apart from his nephew

Teddy.

He expresses a sense of duty towards Teddy, wanting to provide him with a better life than what he had experienced, despite legal constraints under his sisters guardianship.

Tyler doesn't elaborate much further, but his clenched fists and fidgety feet speak volumes about the emotional weight he carries when we talk about his father.

With a second whiskey, Tyler appears visibly relaxed, reclined in his seat with his legs apart, one hand supporting his forehead while the other taps rhythmically on his glass to the beat of the music.

Raising my martini to my lips for a sip, I catch Tyler observing me closely. As I lower the glass, a drop of alcohol escapes down my lip and I swiftly lick it away, biting my lower lip in hopes he didn't see me nearly dribbling.

"Fucks sake, Cass," Tyler arches back into his seat, running his hands through his noticeably greying hair.

My nerves riot under my skin.

"Don't do shit like that, are you trying to turn me on?"

"Excuse me?" I blurt.

"Don't look at me like that," his voice is hushed, as if he's trying not to smile. "You know exactly what it does to me."

He leans forward and his thumb brushes my jaw.

"Cass…I want you. I want to know you. All of you."

He doesn't break eye contact with me.

"I can't stop thinking about you and I don't know how to turn it off."

Tyler lifts his whisky, draining the rest in one quick gulp, then places the glass back on the table.

"Tyler…" My breath catches, like I'm gulping for air. I swallow hard, forcing in a steady breath as I try to collect what's left of my composure.

He pulls my chair closer to him, the green of his eyes dark and smoky. His thumb grazes my left cheek as he tucks my hair behind my ear, his fingers moving further into my hairline.

Pulling my face towards his, he rests his forehead against mine. I close my eyes, his touch sending me into a spiral of desperation.

I want this man.

His fingers delicately trace my scar, and this time, the shivers I feel are no longer that of fear.

Tyler unexpectedly pulls away, stands up and reaches out for my hand.

"Come on. Let's figure this out once and for all".

The room holds its breath.

I reach out and take his hand as he tosses three £50 notes onto the table, leading me towards the exit.

After what feels like the longest twenty-minute drive of my life, Tyler parks outside our flats. Pushing every niggling thought aside, I step out of the car and take a deep breath.

This time, when Tyler comes over to the car door, I reach out for his hand and lead him into my lobby.

Pushing the lift button, I feel my knees tremble slightly.

I know the kind of guy Tyler is and it doesn't change my mind.

I need him.

The lift pings, notifying us of its arrival. Having not spoken a word during the journey here, tension hums through me like a live wire.

Tyler presses me assertively against the lift wall before the doors have a chance to close on us. His warm, alcohol-laced breath caresses my skin, seeking out my lips, as his other hand traces slow deliberate patterns on my thigh, inching higher with quiet intent.

Before I can catch my breath, Tyler lifts me effortlessly, and my legs instinctively entwine around his waist, while my arms drape around his neck, anchoring me there.

As restraint continues to crack, my lips seek his again greedily. My body moulds into his as he presses me further against the lift wall, and his kisses turn breathless as the lift jolts to a stop.

Amidst a flurry of half-broken kisses, Tyler carries me into the corridor towards my flat and I feel every shift of his body beneath me, strong and certain.

My hand trembles as I fit the key into the lock.

This is what I want. Isn't it?

I've spent so long avoiding touch and the danger of being truly known, yet here I am, fingers curling around the door handle, ready to let him see every hidden part of myself – a man who could break me without ever meaning to.

Tyler's lips brush against my ear, his hand steady at my back as if he knows I won't pull away. "I've thought about this moment," he murmurs, his voice rough, barely holding together, "more times than I should have."

The lock clicks and the door swings open.

I barely make it across the threshold before he's kissing me again. Stumbling inside, my fingers find his shirt and I tug him closer, clumsily undoing the buttons one by one, until his broad shoulders and tanned skin are exposed. My mouth finds his neck and my kisses trail lower, down to his chest and Tyler's eyes flutter shut.

I drag my fingertips over his skin, feeling the muscle shift beneath my touch and my breath catches as his control wavers, just for a second, because of me.

My fingers trace along Tyler's torso, catching at the waistband of his boxers.

Tyler stills, his eyes searching mine, and when I don't pull away, he instinctively lifts me and carries me to the bed, his mouth never leaving mine as we cross the room.

He lowers me onto the sheets and hovers above me, bracing his weight on his arms, keeping just enough distance to let me breathe. His hands guide mine above my head, restraining me and a shiver runs down my spine. His mouth curves faintly as if he feels it too.

He lifts my top above my head, slowly, and winds the fabric around my wrists. Not tight enough to hurt, just enough to remind me that I'm not going anywhere.

His lips find my throat, moving slowly, embarking on a journey from my neck down to my breasts, along my torso and my body sinks into my bed.

My fingers knot in his hair, a quiet, desperate admission of need.

Every touch lingers just long enough to keep me on edge, making my heartbeat quicken as I sink further into his soft embrace and for the first time in a long time, I stop bracing for impact.

Tyler is already fast asleep when I slip back into the bedroom, the steady rise and fall of his chest grounding me, as I quietly return to the bed.

My phone buzzes and then stops.

Once, twice, insistent on ruining my night like a bucket of cold water.

I glance at the screen. Multiple missed calls. The phone rings again, and curiosity gets the better of me, so I answer.

"Tell Tyler I said thanks for keeping you warm for me," a voice mutters, slurring slightly.

He ends the call before I find my words, leaving the room too quiet, the softness disappearing with it.

I stare at the call log. Every missed call is from him.

The ex who used to only ever call on my birthday.

CHAPTER 24 - WHEN EVERYTHING CHANGES

The smell of coffee pulls me out of a haze. Walking out of my bedroom, I lean against the door frame and see Tyler leaning against the kitchen counter, a towel loosely tied around his waist.

There's a calmness about him this morning that makes my chest ache slightly. No words, no rush…just him and a sense that something between us has shifted.

"Morning," he says, unguarded.

I wasn't sure I'd ever get used to this sight.

I sip my coffee, letting the memory of last night drift in and out of my thoughts, careful not to give too much away, as though wanting him this openly might tip something delicately out of balance.

He leans against the countertop, one hand bracing himself, the other still clutching the mug. The sunlight catches the edges of his damp hair and I find myself smiling at how ridiculous this is; how easily he can make an ordinary morning feel electric.

"Did you sleep okay?" he asks suddenly, his voice soft. I hadn't expected tenderness this morning. I suppose I'd thought it might be awkward.

"Yeah," I breathe out. I watch him closely, suppressing the

memory of the unwanted calls, hearing a voice I've tried so hard to forget.

"Better than okay, actually."

He laughs softly, the sound rich and warm.

"Good," he says simply and for a moment, there's only the quiet, comfortable weight of knowing we weren't quite strangers anymore.

I stir my coffee, still watching Tyler move around the kitchen. Even in just a towel, he exudes a mix of laid-back confidence and intensity that makes it impossible to look away.

Recalling the moment I woke in the middle of the night, Tyler's arm was wrapped around me; it sent a surge of emotion rocketing through me. It felt right, like I had slipped into a place of belonging.

What if he didn't want this to be anything more than what it was, regardless of his words. What if I'd opened a door he never intended to walk through?

The truth settles heavy in my chest, heavier than I wanted to admit. Tyler made me feel seen in a way that I didn't know I was missing until recently. Safe in a way that both comforted and unnerved me.

Underneath all of that was a deeper realisation, one I wasn't prepared to face, because wanting him meant I'd be risking the balance I'd spent so long building.

"You're staring again," he says, his voice low and teasing, as he leans against the counter near me.

"Maybe," I admit, trying to sip my coffee like it was the most important thing in the world.

He smirks, stepping closer, close enough that I can feel the warmth radiating off him. "I don't mind," he whispers, letting his hand brush against mine as he reaches for the sugar.

"In fact... I kind of like it."

"You... like being watched?" My words brush the air between us.

Tyler's smirk deepens. "Only when it's me being watched," he teases, "And only by you."

A sharp knock on the door interrupts the moment, followed by keys rattling in the lock, and the door swings open before I get the chance to call out.

Lola breezes in like she owns the place.

"Cass! You're not going to believe..."

Her words die mid-sentence as she freezes in the doorway. Her eyes flick between Tyler, in his towel casually leaning against the counter and me, caught somewhere between panic and amusement.

"Oh," her eyes blink slowly. "Right... this is the 'gay' friend you mentioned. The one you've been talking about." I sense a hint of recognition and teasing in Lola's eyes.

Tyler raises an eyebrow, a playful smirk tugs at his lips. "Gay friend?" he repeats, tilting his head in mock curiosity.

My gaze drops to the floor, "Lola..."

"Relax, Cass," she muses, her grin stretching from ear to ear. "I mean, he's cute...but I didn't see that coming!"

Tyler chuckles, clearly enjoying the attention on him, while I hide my face in my hands, silently questioning every life choice that brought me to this moment.

"Well," Lola continues, still standing in the doorway, "I suppose I'll just... leave you two to your... morning coffee, huh?" She winks at Tyler.

Tyler's phone buzzes on the counter. He glances at it, then back at me, a shadow of concern crossing his features.

"I have to go," he says suddenly, voice clipped, eyes catching Lola's. "Something...came up. I'll explain later."

Lola freezes in the doorway.

Grabbing his trousers and T-shirt from the sofa, Tyler dresses swiftly in the bedroom.

"Now?" I ask, surprised.

Tyler gives me a weighted look. "I'll be back. I'll always come back."

Neither has noticed that I've caught on to their lingering glances, and my mind is on the edge of bubbling over.

"Right," I say, stepping fully into my living room. "Everyone in here seems to know things I don't, and it's really starting to piss me off," my voice cracks.

The room stills.

"Cass," Lola says softly, "Can we not do this right now?"

"Do what?" I ask. "Acknowledge the fact you're apparently back from a holiday you never went on?"

"It's nothing," she snaps.

I laugh sharply. "You keep saying that. Funny how *nothing* keeps following you around."

Lola takes a step towards me. "Cass, please. I didn't lie to hurt you."

"But you did lie," I say, quieter now. "You looked me in the eye and told me you were getting on a plane."

Lola remains at the doorway a few seconds too long, arms loosely folded, watching me with an unreadable expression.

Tyler clears his throat. "Girls, I think it's best I leave you two to chat."

I nod, and he takes that as his cue to leave, planting a kiss on the top of my head before shutting the door behind him.

She swallows. "I just needed space."

"From me?" I ask.

Lola exhales shakily. "I panicked. I thought if I kept you out of it, you'd be safe."

"Safe from what?" I ask.

Her eyes well up, but she doesn't answer.

"Safe from what?" I snap.

She swallows. "James said he thought he had seen your ex hanging around recently. I told him I highly doubted it," she pauses, her breath leaving her in a long, burdened sigh. "But… I think he might be right. He hasn't told me much. Hardly anything, actually."

She rubs her forehead with the back of her hand.

They said I was too much of a distraction for you, and that it would be better if I stayed away while they figured things out.

"They?" My breath catches in my throat.

Lola doesn't respond straight away, but she doesn't need to. The truth settles heavily in the room and I realise everyone else has known something I haven't.

"They just needed time to…" She hesitates, "I don't know. Draw him out, maybe?"

My vision blurs as beads of sweat line my forehead, and I lean on the sofa, gripping it until the room steadies.

"You knew who Tyler was this entire time?"

Lola's gaze doesn't reach my eyes but I already have my answer.

Lola keeps her arm tucked tight against her side.

"Lola."

She looks up at me. "What?"

"That bruise," I say. "Tell me the truth."

"I did," she says quickly. "I told you, it was sorted."

"No," my voice remains calm. "You told me a version of what happened, and you didn't let me ask any questions."

She looks away from me and sighs deeply.

I step closer and gently pull her sleeve up before she can stop me. The bruise remains, much fainter than last time, but still unmistakable.

"That bruise is not nothing," I say softly. "And it didn't come from James even though I've had my suspicions."

Lola exhales, long and shaky, like she's been holding her breath.

"I didn't lie," she says. "I just…didn't finish the story," she swallows hard.

"I needed money," she admits. "Not loads, just enough to get ahead. I was behind on rent and I didn't want to ask you because you already do too much," her voice wobbles.

"I didn't think it would be like that."

"Didn't think what would be like that?" I ask relentlessly.

"What it would be like owing the wrong people," she says quietly.

I search Lola's face, but remain quiet so she can finish.

"I agreed to do some favours," she admits.

"What kind of favours Lola?"

She hesitates, shame flickering across her face. "Introductions, being in the right place at the right time, smiling, listening," her eyes meet mine. "Nothing illegal. Nothing I thought was dangerous."

"But it was."

She nods.

"They make you feel stupid and small, like you misunderstood the agreement," her voice drops. "The bruise wasn't punishment, it was a reminder that I can't say no to them."

Rage simmers beneath my skin. "Who are *they*?"

She shakes her head immediately. "No, I'm not dragging you into this."

"You already have," I say gently. "Whether you meant to or not."

Her eyes gloss over. "James stepped in, he was there…" She pauses, "he shut it down and got me out."

"And the people you owe these favours to?"

"They don't like loose ends," she says. "Especially ones who know faces."

Something cold settles in my stomach.

"Lola," I say slowly, "these people…are they connected to Tyler?"

"Not now," she says quickly. "Not like before, but they're from the same circle, from before he cleaned up."

"So, when you said it was sorted…"

"It is," she insists. "James made sure of that."

"For you," I say.

She looks up at me through her eyelashes.

"I didn't know this was going to get so complicated."

I pull her into a hug before she can finish, despite my hands shaking.

"I just wanted things to be easy for once," she says into my shoulder.

My mind races, trying to make sense of the last ten minutes. I've been bait the whole time, and no one thought I deserved to know about any of this. No one thought it would be a good idea to bring me in on the mess.

Lola moves nearer, her hands hesitating before they meet mine. "Alright, Cass," she says softly. "You lied to me too."

I set the empty coffee mug on the counter with more care than it deserves.

"Yes. I lied." The word tastes bitter. "Not on purpose. You question everything, and at the time… I didn't even know what *this* was."

Silence hangs between us like a weight. Lola shakes her head, a small motion, more deflection than amusement.

"So that's your 'gay friend'?"

I cover my face, dragging in a slow breath.

"Seriously though, Tyler is intense. Men like him don't do half measures. They don't let go easily."

I stop and truly look at her, letting my gaze linger.

"He's not like that, Lo. He just…pays attention. More than most people."

Her mouth presses thin, as if she's about to argue, but she knows better.

"Well. That was the world's most creative misdirection. I'm almost impressed." She perches on the edge of my sofa.

"Next time you want me off the scent, maybe just tell me you're hiding a sexy roommate. Less drama."

"Deal." I say, though the relief I'm reaching for never quite arrives.

"You owe me a coffee," she adds, clapping her hands, "and clearly a huge gossip. Chop chop."

Now I understand the truth. The tangled web of lies, and with Tyler and James involved too, this means it wasn't a spur-of-the-moment decision. It was planned. Discussed. Agreed upon…by everyone except me.

How long have they known? Why wasn't I trusted enough to be told?

I feel a storm of a headache brewing while Lola chatters on, her usual charm turned up all the way, but I barely hear a word of it.

If my ex really is back, then maybe I wasn't imagining things after all.

The relief lasts seconds before reality crashes back in.

I'm exposed, like a sitting duck, waiting for the moment someone decides it's my time.

CHAPTER 25 – OLD INSTINCTS, NEW RULES

Tyler

Waiting works until it doesn't.

People often see patience as a virtue when, in fact, it's simply discipline, and discipline is only valuable if you know exactly what you're waiting for.

Saturday morning, I received a text from James asking for me to call him as soon as I left Cass's flat.

Cass knows the truth. She must do after how she confronted Lola. I don't want her to be angry, but keeping her in the dark about all of this has been for her benefit. Surely, she'll understand.

James told me that Cass's ex has been getting more confident and the frequency of the car around the flat has escalated, which means *he's* becoming careless and more erratic.

This morning, I received my confirmation.

James didn't call; he sent a photo of Cass and Lola, laughing outside the cafe, holding shopping bags and drinking coffee.

Sitting in my office at the bar, I feel my grip on restraint slipping.

"They've been out since ten," James says quietly beside me, his voice low enough to blend into the background noise of Sparks Rooftop.

It's now 7:30 pm.

"Nails, coffee, shopping," his eyes focus on his laptop. "The car has been around twice already."

"Same car?" I ask.

"Same car," he confirms.

Cass looks relaxed in the pictures. No heels, hair up. She's laughing with Lola in a way that people do when they're with someone who knows all their faults and loves them anyway, but every so often, her smile falters. Pictures don't lie.

She knows.

I don't interfere...yet. Waiting is still the right call.

James shifts in his seat and I can tell he's sitting on his words.

"Tell me," I command.

It's just that the car isn't near them any longer; it hasn't been for the past half hour. It's parked up near South Street now.

The silence stretches as the pieces slide into place.

"The girls have just left Zara," he discloses. "They're headed straight towards him."

My chair scrapes loudly against the floor as I spring to my feet. I grab my jacket and walk quickly towards the door, adrenaline surging through me, while James fumbles with his car keys.

"We're going on the bike. We'll get there faster, I'm not taking any chances," I respond.

James nods and follows closely.

When we arrive, the car is parked half a street back from where the girls are.

James shifts his weight. "He's been there since before they arrived."

"Which means he knew they were going to come here," I rake

my hand through my hair. "That's not curiosity."

"No," James agrees. "That's fixation."

I don't like the word, but it's true.

Cass steps out first from the little card shop, phone pressed between her shoulder and ear, while Lola is gesturing towards a restaurant behind her, arms laden with shopping bags.

They're about twenty meters away from the car now.

Cass stops in the middle of the street. She doesn't say anything, but hangs up the phone and adjusts her stance, her eyes sweep the road with quiet precision.

Lola leans in, saying something clearly meant to soften the moment and Cass laughs, but it doesn't reach her eyes.

The car that's been idling since we arrived cuts it's engine, as if in response.

That's when my restraint ends.

My body moves ahead of my thoughts and I am already marching towards the car.

Cass and Lola disappear into the Italian across the road as I reach it, leaving no time to think about my actions.

The car door cracks open and I shove it wide, seizing the guy by the collar of his coat.

His eyes widen and his shoulders tense in response.

"What the fu…" His voice trails off as recognition crosses his face.

"You've had a comfortable day," I say calmly. "That ends now."

My hands tighten around his collar, and I drive him back against the open car door. He's smaller than I expected. They always are.

"You don't follow them," I continue, "you don't watch them. You don't sit in cars and pretend to be normal, when you're a fucking creep."

His eyes flick briefly towards the restaurant where Cass is.

His eyes flash with a glimmer of ownership that's been dulled by habit.

"Look at *me*," I snarl, already teetering on the edge of darkness.

He does.

"Leave now," the words rip from my throat. "If I see this car anywhere near here again, I will come for you myself. I will make sure that you regret thinking that you were entitled to even know what they look like," I don't pause to breathe. "You ever fucking see her again, *ever*, I'll come for you personally."

Silence stretches between us.

"Do. You. Fucking. Understand," I spit, not a question, but a warning.

He swallows hard and nods.

I release my grip and he scrambles back into the car.

Dragging my hand through my hair, anger courses through my veins, and I feel James beside me.

Before the car pulls away, a smug smile plays on his face, and his eyes never leave mine. He slams his foot down on the accelerator and disappears into the traffic up ahead.

Cass never saw us and that's important.

"I need a fucking drink," I thunder at James.

James takes my keys without a word, and we head back to Sparks on the bike, the city blurring past beneath the hum of the engine.

I can't relax, so I leave James at Sparks and head back to my flat. I need to know when she gets home.

Just after 9:30 pm Cass returns. Light spills onto her balcony and the door sits slightly ajar, music drifting out in a low thread.

It's a good sign. She's home and blissfully unaware of the events of today.

Even though everything in me wants to head over there to check on her, I don't. I don't call or text either because I want her to have her space.

She doesn't know that her ex is part of something bigger, something linked to me in some way, and even with everything we've uncovered, I still can't quite connect the dots.

I didn't lose control today because, technically it's true.

I stopped short...but only because he drove away.

I felt it, the pull.

I recognised him immediately, the man I used to be. The one who never paused to think about the damage until it was done.

For a second, he was back, close enough that I could feel how easy it would have been to let him take control.

I tell myself I've changed, that I've learnt restraint and I have... but today reminded me that it's not that simple; it's the constant decision *not* to reach for violence.

What frightens me the most is how deeply satisfying it was to stand there again, heart steady, senses sharp, hungry for blood.

Tonight, I'm not congratulating myself for walking away; I'm reminding myself why I must.

CHAPTER 26 - WHEN THE PAST STARTS BREATHING AGAIN

While it was nice to finally catch up with Lola on the weekend, everything that she told me sits heavily on my chest.

It's been tough not having my best friend to rely on when I needed her advice most, and then I discover she's been distancing herself, not because she didn't care, but because she thought it was better for me.

The money, the favours, all of it threads back to the same dark vein Tyler's been circling without ever naming. Lola didn't go out looking for danger; she sought relief and that's what makes my stomach turn the most.

It's not even 7 am and my shoulders already ache under the weight of an invisible boulder.

The reality that it's Monday morning again is all too real. The office buzzes with its usual noise; phones ringing, someone laughing too loudly near the kitchen, but all of it feels strangely distant as I step inside, still replaying the revelations of the weekend.

I tuck a folder under my arm and head towards the conference room, trying to focus on work, though my mind keeps drifting back to the look on Tyler's face before he left.

As I push open the glass door, conversation inside the room

pauses briefly, then carries on. I pretend not to notice, slipping into my usual seat. A few colleagues offer me polite nods, but one person looks a little too long; Harper, from accounting, or am I just imagining it?

Not long after, the door swings open again, and Tyler walks in, calm and professional. His eyes immediately lock onto mine, as if he searched the room for me first.

I straighten in my chair, heat prickling across my skin. He doesn't say a word, but the subtle tightening of his jaw, the shift in his expression, it says enough.

Tyler takes his seat next to me at the table, the perfect picture of calm, but when no one else is looking, his foot brushes mine beneath the table, unmistakably intentional.

"Shall we begin?" he says to the room, voice steady, completely in control.

That small touch under the table makes it clear that whatever had happened this weekend wasn't over. Not even close.

A voicemail notification pops up on my phone from an important client that I have a deadline for this week, so I slip out of the room, politely excusing myself. Part of me is grateful; I need a moment to breathe, a moment without Tyler's eyes catching every flicker of doubt on my face.

I exhale slowly, trying to steady myself, when I hear a voice drifting from the partially open door at the far end.

Luke.

I freeze. I'm not trying to eavesdrop, but his tone is clipped and too tense to ignore. Something is off.

"...Tylers slipping," Luke says, his voice low. "He's distracted. This is the perfect opportunity."

Panic crackles under my skin. I take a careful step forward, angling myself, so the shadows of the hallway swallow me, whilst I edge my way forward.

"I'm not interested in waiting for him to fail on his own," Luke continues. "I need leverage. Something solid."

Leverage. The word twists in my gut.

A muffled voice responds on the other end.

Luke exhales in frustration. "No, not rumours. I need evidence. Something I can present to the board. Something he can't talk his way out of."

This wasn't internal company friction, this was power play.

The other voice says something again, too low for me to catch.

Luke's quiet laugh sends a chill down my spine.

"I know she's close to him," he says. "Of course I know, and if I can't find leverage on him directly, I'll get it through her."

A creeping cold threads through me, inch by inch.

He doesn't say my name, but he doesn't have to. Instinct sends me back a step too quickly. My heel snags the carpet, the faint sound cutting through the silence.

Luke goes quiet and I hold my breath, waiting.

"I have to go. We'll talk later," he says under his breath.

A moment later, his footsteps approach the door and I snap my phone back to my ear, pretending to speak as he steps into the hall.

His gaze fixes on me and he smiles. The kind of smile you only see on men who've already decided how they intend to ruin you.

"Everything alright, Cass?" he asks softly.

I force a smile, although my throat feels tight, as if it's closing around something I cannot swallow.

"Yeah. Just a work call."

He studies me for a moment too long, eyes flickering over my face like he was searching for something he couldn't name.

Inside, my pulse pounds with a truth I can't ignore anymore.

Luke wasn't just ambitious, he wanted to try to get rid of Tyler from the company and he was prepared to use me to get it done.

~

The meeting finally wraps up, papers shuffle, laptops click shut. People filter out of the conference room, exchanging polite goodbyes until it's just me and Tyler.

He leans casually against the table, but his eyes are fixed on me knowingly.

"Cass," he says quietly, voice low so no one else can hear. "Can we talk for a minute? In private."

I nod, my pulse picks up as we step into the empty hallway.

"I need to explain something from the other day," he runs his hand through his hair, his tone even, but careful.

"But I need your word, that whatever I say stays between us."

"Of course," I whisper, risking a brief look around, even though the corridor is deserted. I tug lightly on his arm.

"You've known about *him* this whole time?" My eyes sting as I fight the tears.

He shifts his weight. "It's… complicated."

Footsteps echo behind us and a deep voice cuts in.

"Tyler."

We turn and see Luke standing there. His eyes are cold, and his posture is too stiff to seem casual.

"We need to talk," Luke commands. "Now."

Tyler straightens, a subtle edge sliding into his stance. "Luke. This isn't the time."

Luke doesn't budge. "I don't care," his gaze flits to me, assessing, then snaps back to Tyler.

Tyler steps in front of me protectively. "Cass isn't part of this," he says firmly, "and you don't get to corner me in hallways. If you need a meeting, schedule one."

Luke smirks. "I know how to get your attention. You'll give me what I want, or this drags on."

"No. This is my company. You don't give me ultimatums, and you certainly don't make threats you can't act on," Tyler's hands form fists at his side and then relax.

I feel his hand brush mine.

Luke eventually steps back, hands raised in mock surrender. "Fine. But this isn't over."

Tyler doesn't respond, he just watches Luke until he walks away.

"Let's go," he says softly.

We walk down the corridor together, and my shoulders begin to relax as Tyler's hand stays near mine the entire way. In his office, he leans against the desk, still close enough that warmth pools between us.

"Yesterday... I had to take care of something urgent," he says. "Something involving you."

My stomach churns. "Me?"

He nods once. "Someone from your past. Someone dangerous."

Immediately, my ex flashes through my mind—the pounding on the door, the threats I have tried to bury.

"I'm fighting two battles, Cass," he sighs heavily. "There are people trying to get to me through the company... and through you. I couldn't risk it."

I swallow. "You've been... protecting me? Why weren't you just honest with me." I take a deep breath.

I look into his eyes, searching for his truth.

"Lola told me the truth," I breathe. "She needed money and was pulled into doing favours for people she didn't really understand," I hold his gaze. "People from your old circle."

His eyes darken. "She shouldn't have been anywhere near them."

"No," I agree quietly, "but you helped build the world that made it possible."

Tyler looks away, hand braced on his desk. "Cass..."

"I'm not accusing you," I interrupt. "I'm telling you that I am done being the last person to understand the danger I'm standing in."

The admission lands heavy and my shoulders sag.

"If your past is entwined with our future, then I deserve to know exactly how far it reaches."

Tyler straightens and turns to face me fully.

"I'm sorry Cass... It just wasn't that simple." He runs his hands through his hair again.

"I've had James, Peter, and other members of my security team look through all the details. You lost your ID and bank card that night in Chicago's... the night before we first met. I held onto them so they wouldn't land in the wrong hands," he admits, as he unfastens his suit jacket.

"I know you might be feeling angry and hurt, but everything we held back from you," he pauses, his eyes searching mine. "We did because we care."

A cagey breath escapes me as the room lurches, tilting hard enough to almost steal my footing.

He steps closer, brushing his fingers against mine.

"I didn't want you scared. I wanted to have things handled," he admits.

Unease vibrates through me, but the words I'd been holding in since I'd overheard the conversation in the hallway, burns too hot to ignore any longer.

"Tyler..." I whisper, overwhelmed by his revelation, needing a moment to pull myself together. "I heard Luke earlier."

His expression stills instantly, every muscle sharp and alert.

"What did you hear?"

I hesitate. "He was on the phone. He said he needs leverage on you."

Tyler's jaw flexes, but he remains silent.

"He wants something he can take to the board," I continue, my breath shaky. "Something compromising."

Tyler's eyes darken with confirmation.

"And he said…" My throat tightens. "If he can't find leverage on you directly, he'll find it through me."

Tyler closes the distance between us in a heartbeat, not touching, but close enough for the air to shift.

"Cass," his voice is low and dangerous with restraint.

"I would never let that happen, but I need you to trust me."

I believe him.

A soft knock at the office door startles me.

Tyler's head tilts. "Luke," he mutters, voice tight.

Sure enough, Luke is leaning in the doorway, pretending to be casual, eyes flashing between us with too much interest.

"Everything all right in here?" he asks lightly, though the edge beneath it was unmistakable.

"Yes," Tyler replies smoothly, "and interrupting private meetings isn't how this works. Just schedule the fucking meeting."

Luke smirks. "Noted."

He steps back, leaving the door ajar, like a warning.

I release a shaky breath as Tyler shuts the door behind him, turning the lock.

Even with Luke lingering just beyond the door and shadows from my past resurfacing, one thing was clear: Tyler wasn't just protecting the company, he's been protecting me, and Luke was willing to use that against him.

The thought steals the remaining air from my lungs, and my

chest tightens as panic threatening to spill over again.

Tyler notices immediately and steps towards me.

"Hey," he says quietly, softer now, turning toward me fully. "Look at me."

I try, but the room still feels unsteady. Before I can stop myself, my fingers curl into the front of his shirt and Tyler stills beneath my touch.

His hands come up, firm at my waist, pulling me into him without hesitation.

"I've got you," he says quietly.

The words settle in my mind. I breathe him in, and his hand flexes.

"Cass," he starts, low with warning, but I don't give him time to finish.

I surge forward, catching his mouth with mine in a kiss that's rushed and bruising, pent-up fear and need colliding all at once.

He exhales sharply and kisses me back just as hard. His left hand skims my thigh, lifting me without warning, placing me effortlessly on the edge of his desk as if that's where I belong. His fingers cradle my face, firm but gentle, holding me there like he's afraid to let go.

Tyler pulls back first, his forehead still pressed against mine.

My knees part instinctively as my pulse thumps in my ears. His mouth drifts from mine, tracing the corner of my jaw, lingering close enough to make my skin ache.

"Fuck," he breathes, with more restraint than frustration.

Slowly, Tyler sinks to his knees between my legs as if he's surrendering his power. Like he's choosing me instead.

His hands rest on my thighs, and he tilts his head back to look up at me, his eyes dark with desire.

"You're shaking," he murmurs, his voice rough.

"I'm fine," I lie, because I don't know how to admit I'm not.

His thumbs brush small circles into my skin.

"You don't have to be fine with me," he says, so quietly I can barely hear it over my own breathing.

Tyler leans in, pressing his mouth to my knee first, then up my thigh, in the slowest line of kisses.

I tip my head back, eyes squeezing shut, my hands finding his hair and for a moment the noise in my mind fades. It all goes quiet beneath the way he touches me like I'm worth keeping.

A shuffle of footsteps passes outside the office, bringing us back to reality and Tyler pulls away, resting his chin on my knee, looking up at me again.

"I meant what I said," he says firmly. "I've got you."

Then he stands, his composure sliding back into place, but his hand lingers on my waist a moment longer before he lets go.

CHAPTER 27 - THE WARNING

I don't remember deciding to pour the wine; I just know I've filled it well beyond what I'd usually allow.

My flat is quiet, the kind of silence that presses in on your brain. My thoughts are still trying to catch up with the day and everything that's already gone wrong.

Tyler's words from earlier replay, voice cutting through the stillness as if he's in the room with me.

'There are people trying to get to me through the company and through you.'

I sip my wine, which tastes bitter on my tongue, and an unease settles in my mind as my fingers tap rhythmically against my glass.

Tyler had been calm and collected; the CEO I knew that everyone respected and equally feared. Yet beneath that control lay something far more personal, dangerous even. He had acted to protect me in ways no one would ever know.

What had he done? Had he confronted my ex directly?

I run a hand through my hair, my heart pounding in my chest. Part of me feels grateful, while the other part feels frustrated.

I trust him. Well, I want to, but the secrecy and the weight of his knowledge leaves me feeling powerless.

I turn towards the sofa and halt abruptly.

The blanket I had folded this morning, edges aligned and

corners tucked in, now lies bunched and disturbed on my sofa, in a way that can only mean one thing. Someone's sat there.

I must have forgotten when tidying up earlier. I've been tired…but the blanket isn't how I left it.

My breath shortens, and the walls seem to close in on me. All I want to do is run, but my legs betray me. I'm frozen to the spot.

He's been here.

The skin up to the back of my neck burns, the same spot he once hit and grabbed me. My fingers instinctively trace my scar.

The flowers I received for my birthday, now slightly wilted, sit innocently on the side, almost as if someone had stood exactly where I am now, choosing which flowers would make me shake the most.

Their scent now assaults me, a sickly, sweet mockery. Birds of paradise are my favourite.

My fingers close around the vase as I lift it, the water sloshes, and for a second I swear I can feel the weight of his attention in it, as if he's still here, watching.

I take them over to the bin and drop them in, the flowers crumpling on impact.

I wipe my hands on my thighs, my lungs burning with each breath.

You don't forget what being watched feels like; your skin remembers before anything else.

As I place my glass on the coffee table, something catches my eye, a small slip of paper tucked between the cushions of the sofa.

I freeze, fingers hovering over the note. The handwriting is unfamiliar, deliberate. My stomach clenches.

'Cass,
You need to be careful. Any crazy person could have got in if they really tried. Tyler isn't the man you think he is. He makes deals

no one should trust. Reckless, ruthless and careless, people get hurt when he crosses a line but, he doesn't care. His charm is a mask, a way to manipulate and control and anyone close to him becomes collateral damage. Those who stand in his way disappear or pay the price.'

I swallow hard. My pulse pounds like a drum in my ears.

'Watch closely, trust your instincts, and know that some truths aren't meant to be ignored. The longer you stay close to him, the harder it will be to walk away, or even recognise the danger until it's too late.

I've missed you.'

I stare at the words, heat creeping up my neck, as the room sways around me.

The envelope is unmarked, apart from my name written neatly across the front, so I know it's been deliberately placed there. For a moment, I can't tell whether the spinning is real or if it's just my mind struggling to process the situation.

I sink back onto the sofa, clutching the note tightly.

My mind flicks to Tyler's tattoo, the stormy tree etched into his chest, a symbol of resilience, strength, and perhaps a life lived under constant pressure.

I let this man in; I trusted him, didn't I?

Come on, Cass, trust your instincts.

It's *him*. He's trying to poison the one place, the one person, that makes me feel safe.

Suddenly, every shadow I see feels heavier, as if it's carrying more than just darkness. My flat, which is usually a safe haven, now feels burdened by unseen eyes. He'd been here…in my space. The place I shower, sleep, and have made my own.

I want to call Tyler to tell him what I've found, but a cautious part of me hesitates. Was that what *he* wanted…to draw me out?

The rational part of me tells myself to stay calm. To breathe. To wait. Another part, a small, instinctive part, warns that this is only the beginning.

My sanctuary is no more, replaced by what seems like a crime scene of his mark.

I press the note to my chest as the evening stretches on, my wine long forgotten and my skin prickling with a familiarity I hoped I'd buried for good.

With a heavy sense of knowing, I realise now that he's found me again.

CHAPTER 28 - WHEN THE PAST REARS ITS UGLY HEAD

I wake to a sky drained of light as the sun hides, as if it's complicit in what's to come. The weight of the note is lodged beneath my ribs, heavy as a held breath.

I barely slept; every creak in the flat sounded like proof that someone had been here, and the restlessness seeped into every crack of me, leaving no place untouched.

As I step outside, my nerves are so raw that I flinch at the sudden closing of a neighbour's door, and when I notice a dark car idling across the street, my stomach plummets.

Stopping briefly for a coffee fix on the way to the office, I glance out the window as I wait in the queue.

Across the street, a figure leans against a lamp post, watching.

Panic twists within me, but I force myself to stay still. I tell myself to wait him out, but the truth is, I don't have a choice. My body has already abandoned me, reverting to an old handbook that hadn't been dusted off in years: freeze and survive.

It's been seven years. Seven years since I last saw him, but time doesn't matter; I still recognise the familiar slump of his shoulders, the shadow of a smirk he wore when he thought I wasn't looking.

The version of him that always came before something worse.

The note had warned me to *"Watch closely,"* and now I can't stop watching everything.

I know it's him, I don't need to look twice.

My drink is finally pushed across the counter, and I wrap my fingers around the cup like it's an anchor. I leave with my head down, my pace steady, and I force my body into motion while my mind scrambles behind me.

Outside, the street is bustling and bright, and I don't look back again until I'm halfway to the office.

By the time I reach the building, my coffee feels slippery in my hand. I smile at reception, nodding like I'm fine, as if my entire nervous system isn't screaming.

In the office, Luke won't stop hovering and I keep catching glimpses of that same car near my building, the same shape, the same tinted glass.

I try to tell myself I'm just being paranoid. Trauma brain. The aftershock of someone slipping a note into my home. I catalogue explanations the way I was taught in therapy – breathe, ground, name the fear.

This doesn't feel like paranoia.

This feels intentional, like eyes are lingering just beyond sight.

I don't think I am being watched. I know I am.

By mid-morning, Luke corners me at the coffee machine with the subtlety of a wasp trapped under a glass.

"Rough morning?" he asks, with a polished, oily smile that never reaches his eyes.

"Fine," I waver, forcing my hands not to shake.

"You know," he continues casually, "you might want to keep an eye on your *boyfriend*. The board isn't thrilled. Not with everything that happened with his sister. Shame, really. Shannon always was… volatile."

Tyler's sister is a line no one crosses, yet the way Luke says her name makes my skin crawl.

"What did you just say?" I snap, my hand slamming my mug down on the table, coffee spilling over the sides.

Luke shrugs, more than satisfied with my reaction.

"Just that Tyler comes from a complicated family. It makes the board nervous, especially with old investors circling again."

Old investors. Deals no one should trust. Reckless. Ruthless. People get hurt.

The words from the note slam into me again.

"Luke," I say tightly. "What do you want?"

His smile sharpens. "For Tyler to stop pretending he's untouchable. For him to remember he's replaceable and for you..." he taps my arm lightly, "...to stay out of things you don't understand."

He turns on his heels, leaving me with my pulse hammering.

Tyler arrives precisely at 3:33pm, his entrance cutting through the office hum while I'm on the phone with a client. He doesn't glance my way or slow, he just walks down the corridor purposefully, heading straight into one of the meeting rooms.

My foot taps the floor, eager for the call to end. I hurriedly offer reassurances, promise callbacks I barely hear myself make, and the moment the line clicks off, I head to the far end of the office, pausing at the corner.

Voices drift from the meeting room ahead.

"You shouldn't have let this go on," Luke says.

"Remind me again why this is any of your concern Luke," Tyler replies sharply.

"I've reviewed the files, her history. I've seen it all."

"Files you had absolutely no right rifling through to begin with," Tyler's voice rises.

I press my palm to the wall for balance.

"If that information surfaces, that her ex is linked to all sorts of shit," Luke continues, "the board won't ask questions, they'll remove you."

A chair scrapes loudly on the floor.

"I think you're forgetting who owns this business," Tyler snaps. "You don't get to decide who I am involved with."

Luke exhales slowly. "I suggest you think carefully about where your priorities lie," Luke adds, "before I'm forced to remind everyone of who I am to this business."

My heart hammers in my chest as I stand paralysed against the wall.

Tyler's voice cuts back in. "Go on," he says. "Tell them. Tell everyone how your Mum spread her legs for my deadbeat Dad, and the only reason you're still standing is because of the deal we agreed with him, because he felt sorry for you."

Silence follows. The kind that follows a truth no one wanted spoken.

I step back. Whatever broke in that room isn't something I can ignore hearing. I turn before either of them can open the door and catch me standing there.

I walk into the kitchen and make a cup of coffee because it's something to do with my hands. I pour it down the sink as soon as it's ready and grasp the edge of the counter until the shakes pass. Caffeine won't help, it'll just make me more jittery.

I return to my desk, and Tyler's office door is shut, so I knock quickly before letting myself in without waiting for a response.

He's sitting at his desk, staring blankly at a pile of papers but clearly not seeing any of them. He doesn't look up when I walk in.

"What did Luke say to you today?" he asks quietly.

I stop just inside the doorway. "He mentioned your sister," I say carefully.

Tyler's body stills. "What else?"

I step closer, the air heavy with unspoken words. "Tyler... what happened?" My voice softens despite my inner turmoil. "With Shannon? With all of this?"

I click the door shut behind me.

"I can't keep guessing," I say, covering my eyes with my hands, my brain exhausted.

"Not any longer. Both of our pasts have come back to haunt us with a vengeance we can't ignore, and I don't know how much more of this I can endure." I draw in a breath, the sound rough in my throat.

He finally raises his head. His eyes are darker than I've ever seen, almost haunted.

"My sister got involved with people she shouldn't have," he says quietly. "Dealers. Men who used her. When she got pregnant, those same people threatened her and my nephew. At the time I had money but not enough power to push them out. So, I made deals. Stupid, desperate deals to keep them alive."

The note's words echo again in my head.

"Tyler..." I whisper.

"And I'm still cleaning up the mess."

My phone buzzes, stealing my attention.

Unknown number. One picture attachment.

My stomach lurches.

It's a photo of me, taken that morning, as I was leaving my flat.

'You shouldn't have walked away from me. You won't make that mistake again.'

My hand shakes violently. Tyler notices and softly reaches for my wrists.

"Cass, look at me."

I step back, breath stuttering, not from Tyler, not from fear, but from the sharp, burning realisation rising in my chest.

"Cass," Tyler says again, firmly this time. "Look at me. ...I know about your ex, the calls, the note," his eyes burn, "I have him being tracked. He will not get to you."

His words should soothe me, but instead, when I look at him, it only makes things worse, the fear of what my truth would force him into. The fear of watching him walk away once he understands the mess I carry.

His hands close around my shoulders tenderly.

"You are not alone," he says softly.

"We'll get through this together," he says confidently. "Don't do anything stupid. We've worked so hard to get to this point. Promise me."

I say nothing. I nod and leave Tyler's office.

For the first time since the note appeared, I feel steady. I won't run. Not any longer.

CHAPTER 29 – I WON'T LET HER WALK ALONE

Tyler

Cass thinks that she's being careful.

That's the danger with people who have survived something once: they confuse self-reliance with safety. They convince themselves that doing it alone is a sign of strength.

Sometimes it is, and sometimes it's merely habit disguised as courage.

I know she's going to leave before she does.

It's not because I'm watching her every move, I'm not, but because she doesn't ask enough questions; she accepts what I've told her too easily.

People preparing for confrontation don't want witnesses.

As she steps out of my office, insistent that she wants to go home later to make everything make sense, my phone vibrates in my pocket.

The hours crawl by, sour and unresolved, filled with a hope that she trusts me… that she won't do anything stupid.

James calls before I can.

"She's in a cab," he says, "but her phone's turned off."

I clench my hands into fists; I hate not being in control of the situation, but I have to trust her, or at least pretend I do.

"Where to?" I ask.

There's a pause. "Ashcroft House."

A development we recently tendered for, which is still under construction, isolated, and empty.

I hang up.

I don't rush because rushing causes you to miss things, and now more than ever, I need to stay sharp.

'Stay back unless I say otherwise.' I tap out to James before sliding my phone into my pocket.

I don't need to tell him where I'm going, he already knows.

It's only 6:30 pm, but the city tonight looks sharper than usual. I weave my bike through motorway traffic calmly, as if I'm riding without purpose.

My heart disagrees.

I keep my breathing even, but the moment my thoughts drift to what's at stake, to the fact that the threat is real, my speed hitches up a notch.

Cass doesn't want saving, but she can't do this alone, even if she hates me for deciding that.

The building comes into view just as my phone buzzes again. I switch off the engine early, coasting the last stretch. I don't like being seen when I don't have to be. I park the bike near a rusted container at the edge of the yard and slip into the shadows, instinct taking over.

If crossing a few lines is the price of keeping her safe, I have already decided I will pay it.

It hits me then, I've been relying on him being alone here all along. Betting on it, but if he's part of something bigger... what if I'm outnumbered?

What if she is.

I shut the thought down immediately. Weakness isn't an option right now, neither is fear.

I move faster, scanning and making notes of exits and blind spots. I want eyes on them before things tip too far.

Voices rise just before I reach the corner of one of the half-built blocks, his first, the low and calm, one that knows exactly which buttons to press because he installed them.

Cass's voice answers back, steady and controlled.

Pride swells in my chest, sudden and fierce. She's standing her ground.

A dull thud sounds, the clash of skin against skin, and her cry stops me cold. I move before I have a chance to think.

I storm into the shell of a room as it leans towards chaos, boots crunching on the concrete. Cass is upright but shaking, he's stepping too close to her and something within me stirs awake.

My body welcomes the feeling like an old friend, one I believed I'd buried years ago.

The line gives beneath my feet and this time I don't pull back; I let the part of me that knows how to finish things take over.

CHAPTER 30 - THE CONFRONTATION

I spend the second half of my day in a haze I can't shake. Voices blur together, with every muscle tensed for impact.

He's been circling the edges of my life again, this time with more personal and intense threats. The sick familiarity of feeling trapped gnaws at me. History has shown me exactly what he's capable of.

I've spent years convincing myself I'm safe, yet here I am again, watching my breath, swallowing panic, fighting memories that don't stay buried.

The thought of confronting him knots my stomach so tightly, and bile rises. I barely make it to my bin in time.

What unsettles me most is the way he feeds off my reactions and my fear, but avoidance hasn't helped me either, and silence has only given him space to imagine himself welcome in my life.

I don't go home after leaving the office.

I jump into a cab through the city instead, streets blurring past me with my mind stuck on one truth; I am finished letting him have control of me.

The next message comes just after 6:15 pm.

'Come to Ashcroft House. Now. Alone.'

My stomach lurches, but this time fear doesn't knock me down; instead, it steadies me, daring me onward.

I don't text anyone. I don't warn Tyler because, for the first time, the decision is entirely mine.

Ashcroft House is a half-built development that we have put tenders in for at Sparks Developments. A skeletal structure, with glass still to be installed, each window a dark, gaping mouth. Concrete and exposed steel beams surround me, stairwells leading to nowhere, letting the wind whistle freely through them.

Every instinct in me screams to turn around, but I am so endlessly tired of running.

It all feels wrong. Too still. As if the walls themselves are hiding their own secrets. Every instinct I was trained to ignore rises in a nauseating wave. I try to tell myself that I am not that girl any more, but my body remembers, and yet... I keep walking.

Tyler's face flashes in my mind, along with his worry and certainty that I am not alone in this.

The wind whistles through the exposed beams as I step into the derelict building.

"You came," a voice says behind me.

I turn and there he is.

My ex stands, leaning against one of the concrete posts, barely lit by a solitary street lamp. His hair is shorter, his face older, but his eyes are exactly as I recall; cold and cruel.

"You never did know how to stay gone," he says stepping forward.

"Or you really didn't try at all. Admit it, you just wanted me back, but you enjoy the chase of it all too much," his voice slurs slightly.

I don't move.

"I'm not here for you," I spit, adrenaline keeping me upright. "This needs to end."

He laughs, venom seeping through.

"You think you decide that? You think walking away from me

was the end?" His jaw clenches. "You shouldn't have made me come find you."

He moves quickly, faster than I anticipate, twisting my arm back and shoving me against a concrete pillar.

My breath stutters as old terror rises.

His grip tightens around my wrist, his voice brushes my ear, but fear doesn't take hold.

"Let go of me you bastard!" I shout without a shake in my voice, his hand full of my hair, pulling tighter.

He smirks. "Still pretending you're something without me."

His palm connects with my face before I have a chance to realise what's happened, and I let out a cry as my breath escapes me.

Another voice tears across the empty building, echoing through me.

Tyler.

He steps into view. Chest heaving, eyes dark with fury, and the mask he usually wears has slipped.

My ex's grip tightens, pleased at Tyler's arrival. "I always knew he'd come running," he says lightly. "I just thought it'd be sooner to be honest."

"Let her go," Tyler growls. "Now."

My ex smiles slowly. "Funny thing," he says, flicking his gaze between us. "You don't even know what game you are up against, do you?"

Tyler doesn't answer. His eyes remain fixed on the hand in my hair, fists clenched. He's assessing, holding himself together through sheer will.

My ex leans closer to me, voice lifting just enough for us both to hear.

"Have you ever noticed how people like him always turn up after the damage has been done?"

Tyler stiffens. "What are you talking about?" hee snaps. "I told you once before to stay the fuck away."

My ex chuckles. "Ask him about the people he used to work with. The kind who buy silence. Who use men like me until we're no longer useful."

Tyler's jaw tightens and confusion flickers briefly.

"You don't know a fucking thing about me," he snaps, his words landing defensively.

"Cass," Tyler says firmly, eyes never leaving *him*, "he's trying to get in your head."

"No," my ex snarls, yanking me forward, fingers digging into my scalp right where the scar burns and my scream rips out of me like a crack of thunder.

"He's lying," my ex hisses. "Same way he always lies. Same way he lets people get hurt and walks away clean."

Tyler exhales once, slow and controlled; the sort of breath someone takes after accepting what's to come.

Tyler lunges, moving with the familiarity of someone who has done this before and knows how to ensure it never comes back to him.

My ex lets me go just in time to face Tyler head-on; the two of them crash to the ground. Fists, elbows, and blood fly everywhere. It all blurs in a violent tangle.

"STOP!" I scream, but it falls on deaf ears.

My ex reaches for something; metal glints under the flickering street light. A knife.

I feel my world narrowing into a single point, his hand in my hair, the sting along my scar, the echo of a scream that belonged to a version of me I refused to be anymore.

Beneath the fear, something else rises. Anger. Hot anger. A surge of clarity that slices through every memory he ever tried to possess. I wasn't frozen. I wasn't small. Not anymore.

I seize the nearest item, a broken metal pole lying beside a stack of discarded plasterboard, and swing it with all my strength, hitting him hard around the head.

The knife clatters away into the shadows and he clutches his head.

He turns towards me, eyes blazing, blood trickling down his face, his feet unsteady.

"You little BITCH!" He lunges at me.

I don't freeze this time.

I push him back with the pole, hands trembling but firm. "I'm not scared of you," I say, breathless.

He snarls and charges again, but Tyler grabs him from behind, pulling him down.

Sirens wail nearby as my ex thrashes, screaming my name like it's still his to own, but I stand there, chest heaving, my pulse drowning out all external noise.

Tyler looms over him like a man coming undone. He grabs the collar of my ex's jacket and hauls him up just long enough to strike. The blow lands with a sickening crunch, bone against bone, and he collapses to the floor, folding the wrong way, as blood begins to seep slowly across the concrete.

The sound does it, it rips straight through me.

For a moment I'm somewhere else entirely, my ears are ringing, and I feel that familiar, blooming pressure at the back of my head.

I remember the confusion more than the pain, the way my fingers kept coming away wet no matter how hard I pressed on the back of my head. How my hands shook with fear, and my clothes were stained red.

I don't flinch. I never did.

I remember how quickly I learned not to, how silence was the difference between surviving and worsening things.

I replay all the times Tyler's been careful with me, the restraint, the softness. He's spent so long keeping this side of him hidden away, buried under suits and schedules. It wasn't because it was gone; it was because he didn't want me to see it.

As the police arrive and drag my ex away, the world doesn't snap back into place immediately. It comes in fragments: police radios chattering, Tyler breathing somewhere behind me, the crunching of gravel. Relief hasn't arrived yet.

Tyler, bruised, blood seeping from a cut above his eyebrow, makes his way over to me.

"What you just saw..." Tyler says quietly, "he didn't give me a choice."

I don't respond, my eyes drift from the blood-stained patch to my own hands once more.

"You hurt him," I whisper. "Badly."

"Yes," he doesn't soften it. "And he still gets to live, that's remorseful enough."

"I had it under control," I breathe, panic leaking beneath my words.

"No, you didn't Cass," he says firmly.

Silence stretches between us.

"I didn't tell you where I went. How did you find me?"

"You didn't have to," he says, running a hand through his blood-matted hair.

"I told you, I've had James monitoring him for a while now," tugging up his shirt sleeves, "I wasn't going to take any risks with you, I was always one step ahead."

My heart sinks.

"So, this is who you are?" I ask, hands trembling at my sides, feeling impossible to still.

He pauses. "This is a part of me," he says carefully. "One I don't use unless there's no other option," he sighs. "And tonight, you were in danger."

"That scares me, Tyler," I admit, searching his face for remorse, but I don't find it.

He steps back, creating space between us. "I don't want you to be afraid of me. I want you to know I'll always protect you," his voice roughens. "But you shouldn't have come alone tonight."

"I had to, I had to stop running," I respond, the words coming out steadier than I expect.

His eyes soften, pride and love all tangled together.

"You protected me," he says, almost in disbelief.

I breathe, truly breathe. I push aside the mark of the chaos still humming in my bones and reach for him, fingers brushing his cheek.

"And for once… I protected myself too."

CHAPTER 31 - HOLDING THE FRAGILE PARTS

The hospital smells of antiseptic. Tyler lies in the bed, stitched and bandaged but safe, his breathing steady. He drifted off an hour ago, and I haven't moved from the chair beside him.

It didn't hit me straight away. Not when the nurse took his blood pressure, not even when the doctor stitched up the cut above his eye, but now, watching his chest rise and fall, over and over, my hands begin shaking.

I tuck them into my sleeves, pressing my palms together, attempting to ground myself in the present.

I tell myself I'm safe, but anger slips in regardless.

The way Tyler moved keeps replaying in my mind. The ease of it, the way he decided for me what would happen next.

I understand why he did it, and that understanding coils tight in my chest, uncomfortable and complicated. Part of me is furious that he took that choice away from me. Another part, a truth I'm finding harder to admit, is grateful he did.

The contradiction makes my head throb.

I look at him again and feel everything all at once: fear, relief, resentment, and something dangerously close to tenderness. My body doesn't know which reaction it's supposed to settle on, so it holds onto all of them instead.

I reach out before I have time to think better of it, my fingers hover for a second before they gently settle against the back of his hand.

How am I meant to reconcile the man I've come to know with the one who crossed the line for me tonight?

When Tyler's eyes finally blink open, I release a breath I hadn't realised I'd been holding.

"Hey," he murmurs.

"Hi," I whisper.

"Cass..." He swallows hard. "I'm sorry for everything I dragged into your life. For every deal I made trying to protect my nephew, for not telling you sooner. I should've handled this better."

"You protected your family," I say gently before he can spiral.

"And I should've protected you better too," he groans, eyes squeezing shut.

I shake my head. "I don't need saving anymore."

A small smile pulls at his mouth. "I noticed."

I lace my fingers with his, and his grip tightens instinctively, as if he's anchoring himself.

I lower my hands slowly and meet his eyes.

"I know about Luke," I say quietly. "I know who he is to you. I know why he's still here and why he thinks he has the right to threaten you."

Tyler's mouth opens slightly like he's going to say something, but he doesn't.

"I know about your father and his mother..." I sigh.

"Luke isn't a problem you manage, he's a reminder you can't cut loose without tearing something open."

I take a breath that hurts on the way in.

"And I know he's been digging into my past because he thinks if he proves I'm a liability, he can force you out without ever touching you directly. So don't tell me this is just business and it's contained, because it isn't. It's all connected: Luke, my ex, your sister, the choices you made before I ever walked into Chicago's, and whether you meant to or not, I'm standing right in the middle of it and always have done."

Tyler remains still for a long moment; he just looks at me as if he's weighing up his answer.

Then he nods. "Yeah," he says quietly.

The simplicity of his response steals my breath.

"Luke's my brother," he continues, voice flat. "Not by blood, not legally but by consequence." He glances away.

"My father took his mother apart and left her with nothing but a name she couldn't use. Luke grew up knowing exactly where the line was, close enough to touch what was taken from him, but never close enough to own it."

Tyler places his other hand on top of mine and squeezes gently.

"He doesn't want me out because of you," Tyler adds, "he wants me out because I built something that didn't include him."

His gaze finds mine once more. "You're merely the lever he believes will finally shift the weight."

I swallow hard.

"I should have told you sooner," Tyler confesses, "but the moment I did, I wouldn't have been able to keep you out of it."

There's so much I want to ask him, about what my ex said, about the things he implied, the way he spoke like he knew Tyler, and the way Tyler came undone tonight.

But not here, not like this.

"I should have been honest with you sooner too. We'll figure everything out later. Right now, you need to rest."

Tyler nods, his eyes fluttering shut again, but my mind doesn't rest with him.

Five Days Later

In the days that follow, everything moves quickly.

My statement is taken twice, once at the hospital and again at the station with a different officer. The same questions are asked, as if they're checking my story.

They tell me he's being charged. That the messages alone are enough to prove a pattern of behaviour and then, quietly, they tell me there's another woman.

They don't give me her name. They say it's due to confidentiality and protocol, but all I hear is the part that matters.

He is remanded in custody while they process the charges.

Relief comes in small, broken pieces. I manage to sleep more than two hours at a stretch the night after the incident, four hours at most in the days afterwards. The first time I step outside, I don't scan every car or startle at my shadow.

Work moves around me like nothing has happened because nothing ever pauses for anyone's trauma. Projects carry on and tenders are reviewed, but I notice the difference.

Extra security measures around Sparks, with site visits requiring two people to be present at all times.

And Luke...

Luke's absence was noticeable in the office.

His name vanishes from meeting invites, his clients quietly relocated to other team members. No announcement, no explanation.

Rachael mentions it in passing while we're filing reports.

"HR's reviewing some irregularities tied to this file," she says. "Luke's been placed on permanent leave." She takes the folder from my hands and shrugs. "Board decision."

I nod casually, keeping my expression neutral, but my insides sigh with relief.

Whatever he thought he had on Tyler never found its teeth, or maybe it did and someone decided it couldn't be allowed to bite.

By the end of the week his name is removed from the internal directory.

Luke wasn't pushed out of a job; he was cut loose from a family that tolerated a borrowed seat, for a place that was never truly his.

In The Weeks After

The courthouse is colder than I expect, dark and lifeless.

Since the arrest, everything unravelled faster than I could brace myself for. Two statements, two women. Years of messages and photos laid bare like evidence of a life I didn't even know I was still living.

He plead guilty at the first hearing.

I still don't know who the other woman is. The police wouldn't tell me, but her statement changes everything. It's no longer just about what he did to me. It's a pattern.

My ex is led in by officers, his wrists cuffed as they guide him towards the dock. His face is still healing, bruises yellowing at the edges, and the craziest part of it all, he looks smaller in here. Less like the monster that lurked in the corner of my memories and more like a man who built himself up out of ego.

He won't look at me, but I don't look away.

The sentencing feels surreal, with years of fear compressed into minutes. The judge's voice drones through the chamber, listing offences: two victims, prior history, patterns, psychological harm, physical harm, risk of repetition.

"Five years imprisonment."

My eyes close instinctively. That's it. A lifetime of damage, and he's only gone for five years.

Lola grips my hand tight. Maddie leans against me.

"It isn't enough," I whisper.

"No," Lola agrees softly. "But it's something and he didn't win."

Opening my eyes, my ex is staring straight at me. Smiling. A small, sinister curve of his lips, as if he knows more than I do, and the scar at the back of my neck throbs, finally revealing the truth.

Some people don't stop being dangerous just because you survive them.

As we exit into the hallway, a voice stops me.

A woman stands a few feet behind me, hands twisting together.

"I was in the courtroom.... I used to date him," her voice cracks. "I tried to leave and he... I never thought anyone else would understand."

I stop to look at her.

Her fear and shame twist into each other, things I recognise all too well.

"I understand," I say softly. "And you don't have to face this alone, please don't be alone. Here..." I hand over my business card since that's all I have on me.

"I'm free to talk anytime."

Her eyes fill with tears. "Thank you."

As she leaves, something settles within me, not quite peace, but purpose.

I feel Tyler shift beside me. "You did good," he says quietly.

As we approach the exit, Tyler's hand hovers for a moment at my back like an unspoken question. I nod, and he rests his hand there. The familiar spark of electricity runs through me, but my ex's smile remains, etched in my mind like a bruise that won't fade.

I am not what he made me. I survived him and now, perhaps, I can help someone else survive too.

CHAPTER 32 - INTO THE FIRE WITH OPEN EYES

Tyler doesn't take me to the flat across the road. He takes me somewhere different.

A quiet street lined with old oak trees, their branches stretching overhead like they're keeping watch. Soft brick houses sit close together, familiar and peaceful. He unlocks the door and steps aside, allowing me to go in first.

Gentle warm light welcomes me. Books are cluttered on shelves and tables, their spines worn from frequent handling and reading. A brown sofa sits in the centre of the room, well-used and comfy, adorned with scatter cushions that look inviting.

It smells like home. Not mine, but his, and somehow that feels like an invitation.

Family photos line one wall, some with Shannon before everything fractured. One of his nephews catches my eye; he has a missing tooth and a grin that's too big for his face.

Something in my chest loosens a fraction.

"This is your real home," I whisper, the words landing softly.

He nods, his voice low. "I didn't show you before because... it mattered too much."

For the first time I can remember, the quiet doesn't feel empty and I turn to him.

"Tyler... I want to try with you properly. No running. No secrets," I pause momentarily. "If you want that too."

He doesn't hesitate to reply, stepping closer to me.

"I want everything with you..." his voice softens further. "There's no future I want that doesn't involve you"

He plants a grounding kiss on my forehead. "Now, can I tell you the next step?"

I lean into him, looking up into his eyes. "Go on then."

Tyler reaches into his pocket, not for a ring but for a small, singular golden key and places it in my palm.

My breath catches. "Tyler..."

"It's yours if you want it. All of it. Not because I expect you to move in tomorrow, just because I want you to know you belong somewhere you're safe. I want to *know* you're somewhere safe."

My fingers close around the key. "I'm ready," I say, my voice steady.

He exhales, leans in, and kisses me slowly and unhurriedly, like a promise rather than desire.

Later, curled against him on the sofa, with lights shining through the window, I receive a text from the girl I'd met in the courthouse earlier that week.

Unknown number: '*I can't tell you how freeing it feels knowing that prick is finally behind bars and it's because of you. Hope you don't end up regretting giving me your number.*'

A second text follows.

Unknown number: '*Oh its Liv, from the courthouse by the way, you know... well of course do you. Speak soon xx*'

Smiling softly at my phone, Tyler reads the message over my shoulder and gives my hand a reassuring squeeze.

"You're incredible, Cass."

I smile into his chest. "I guess I just know what it feels like to be her," I shrug lightly.

Maybe I'm just finally allowed to become who I was always meant to be, someone who survived, who has had the strength all along.

"Oh, I forgot to mention," Tyler whispers into the top of my head, "the deal is ours, construction for the new-build starts next month and the client wants us to represent them."

"I just knew it would be ours," I plant a kiss on his lips and linger, unwilling to rush something that finally feels certain.

The night settles around us, warm and quiet, and for the first time, I don't feel on edge. I feel at home with him, with myself, and with everything still ahead of us.

One Month Later

The house is warm and calm, filled with soft light filtering through the open kitchen windows, allowing the faint scent of Tyler's aftershave to drift through the air. Standing at the kitchen counter, I'm sorting paperwork for the new development project we are heading.

I know I deserve this peace, but I'm still learning to trust it.

A knock sounds at the door, three sharp taps. Tyler looks up from his laptop. "Expecting anyone?"

"No."

Old instincts drag themselves out of hiding.

Tyler crosses the room and opens the door, cautious but unalarmed. A single envelope lies on the mat outside our front door.

No stamp. No name. No return address.

He frowns as he picks it up. "It's probably for the neighbours, they always seem to get us mixed up..."

"Give it to me," I urge quietly.

A silent knowing slithers through me, one that doesn't need to be spoken. My fingers shake as I slide a nail beneath the flap and pull out a single piece of paper.

Four words.

I'll see you soon.

Tyler's expression breaks; fury, protectiveness, and fear clash all at once. "Cass..."

"It's okay," I whisper, folding the paper carefully, anchoring myself in the precision of it.

"He wants me scared," I pause. "He wrote it from prison."

I meet Tylers eyes, my voice holding steady, surprising even me.

I take a lighter from the kitchen drawer and hold the strip of paper over the kitchen sink, setting fire to one of the corners. I release it and watch it curl and blacken.

Tyler moves behind me, arms wrapping around my waist. "Whatever comes, we'll face it together."

I lean back into him, my gaze still fixed on the burning paper. My heart neither races nor breaks.

He didn't write fear into those four words; he wrote certainty. A message meant for me, but a threat for someone else entirely.

"I know, but this time I'm not the one who should be afraid."

I don't look away from the burning letter.

The weight of what came before still hasn't loosened its grip, and I am not prepared to let it win.

ACKNOWLEDGEMENT

This book was written with more late nights, messy
emotions and glasses of wine than I care to admit.
To everyone who stood by me through the constant
"I still have a few chapters to write," thank you.
To my Sister, Mum and Tony who support me
in whatever madness I try next.
To all my friends who read early drafts, late drafts and my
numerous plot changes and didn't judge me for the chaos.
To my Dad, thank you for loving me so deeply. Losing
you so suddenly broke something in me that will never
quite heal. You believed in me without needing to
understand what I was creating and you would have
been impossibly proud to see this become real.

Finally, to every reader, few or many at all - Thank
you for picking up this story and for giving these
characters a home beyond my own mind

ABOUT THE AUTHOR

Jessica Lipani

Jessica writes romance for readers who believe love isn't always gentle, but it can be healing.

Her stories explore connection in the most vulnerable form: the kind that forms after survival, where trust is tentative, desire is complicated, and safety is something that has to be learned.

She is drawn to emotionally intense relationships, quiet devotion, and the moments where two people choose each other despite the weight of what came before.

The Weight of What Came Before is her debut novel written during a season of profound personal loss and change. This is the first book in a trilogy exploring how the past shapes us and how love, loss, and survival leave their mark long after the danger has passed.

It reflects her fascination with resilience, guarded hearts, and the kind of love that doesn't erase the past but stands beside it.

When she isn't writing, she's listening to music that matches her mood, whilst finding meaning in the quiet moments of everyday life with family and friends.

Printed in Dunstable, United Kingdom